ABIGAIL DARE

For my wife, a paragon of restraint.

Abigail Dare

Copyright © 2012 by Jon Etheredge

Third edition, October 2012
Second edition, July 2012
First edition, April 2011

The characters and events in this book are fictitious or of historical significance.

Jon
Etheredge

ABIGAIL DARE

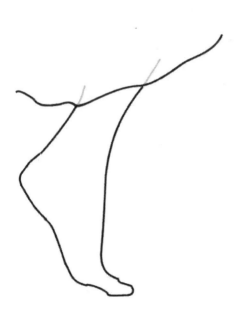

There's no such thing as ghosts.

ᕦ CHAPTER ONE ᕤ

When Myra Luckworth discovered the old house was on the
market, she almost jumped out of her wheelchair. It had been
two years since Abbie wandered off and died. Two years of
listening to the nurses at the Regency go on and on about that
crazy old woman as if she were some kind of saint. *Idiots!*
Oh, she had such delicious plans for this house!

Myra was a resident at Regency Nursing, just as Abbie had
been when she was alive. She chose to live at the Regency
because she liked it better than the other nursing homes, and
because she was vile and despite her money, nowhere else
would take her.

Her taxi parked in front of the Dare house at exactly noon.
The driver pulled Myra's wheelchair from the trunk, unfolded
it and helped her slide over. The realtor, Besse Mervis, tipped
him five dollars to stick around and help push the chair.

"Shall we go in?" she asked the group.

"No need," Myra said. "Tell me about the foundation.
What's underneath?"

Besse hesitated to answer, so Myra impatiently rephrased
the question. "Well is it steel beam or stone or wood or what?
What's holding the place up?"

"Oh, the foundation! Now, keep in mind I haven't
actually been *under* the house, but I do know that the central
fireplace sits on top of a natural boulder, and the house itself is

set atop hand-hewn and individually set oak beams. The walls have oak studs throughout…"

"I didn't ask about the damn studs. How much asbestos?"

"Asbestos? Let me see," Besse flipped through her inspection report. "No, there's no mention of asbestos."

"Good. That means it'll be cheaper to burn it down," Myra said. "More fun, too."

"*Burn* it? Burn it *down*? Did I hear you right?"

"Damn straight. I'm gonna set fire to it and get my dozer man to shove the ashes into a trench."

"But why? It's such a beautiful old house."

"It sure is. Let's go look around inside while we still can. Then I'll talk your price down twenty percent and write you out a check." She stabbed at the front door with a knobby finger, signaling the taxi driver to pull her up the stairs.

There was plenty of room inside the hallway to turn the wheelchair around without hitting anything. Just inside and on the left, a pair of glass-paned double French doors stood open, forming a cavernous passageway into the living room. As the cabbie pushed her through, Myra noticed a change in the air.

The walls were freshly painted, but her nose picked up something else, something from long ago. "What is that odor?" she asked.

Besse sniffed the air and shrugged. "What odor, Miss Luckworth?"

"I don't know, it's so faint, it's…it's maple. I smell maple!" She twisted in her chair and faced the kitchen. The aroma was stronger from that direction. "It's coming from over there." She pointed toward the kitchen door, and when the taxi driver was slow to obey she gripped the hand rims and rolled the wheels herself, advancing through the dining room and into the kitchen.

It was a grand old kitchen. From deep inside Myra, happy memories woke up and spilled out in a torrent of words. "When I was a little girl, my family vacationed in Vermont and we always had griddle cakes on Saturday morning. Not pancakes. We didn't call them pancakes, not my family! We filled up on *griddle* cakes." She paused to breathe, sighing from the effort of remembering so much. "Griddle cakes, with lots of fresh, hot maple syrup!"

Besse was talking on and on, gesturing at a brick hearth, pointing at a cabinet. Myra didn't hear a word. The kitchen had swallowed Myra with its promise of happier times. She could practically hear the metallic clink and tink of forks and knives and plates and coffee cups filled with orange juice. The odor of maple was stronger in the kitchen, as though someone had recently spilled syrup on the griddle.

It was an old, burned-in smell, an odor she had gladly forgotten, a sharp caramel scent digging at her nose, itching inside and telling her that something was wrong. Bad wrong.

She could hear the recriminations echoing off the walls, accusing, biting. You don't put syrup on griddle cakes until they're OFF the GRIDDLE! What's WRONG with you girl? What were you THINKING about?

The scent changed slightly, deepening with a gray hint of pancakes left to cook far too long, the smoke burning her eyes as her parents shouted hate words at each other. She wanted to leave the kitchen, *now!* Her chest pounded with the shame of running away but she couldn't stop the smell and she couldn't stop the voices and she couldn't stop.

Myra rolled herself back into the dining room. The smell had grown worse out here – oppressive, sticky and thick. Her head ached and she burped, surprising herself with the smell of blackened maple syrup.

Unable to stand the burnt stench, she held her breath and retreated, rolling into the living room. The smell of burning syrup was far heavier than before. It stuck to her clothes and her hands and clung to her hair.

Memories of a breakfast long ago, that morning in Vermont when she last saw her father, filled her eyes with maple-flavored tears that made it impossible to find the way out. Myra was suddenly lost and alone and trapped. Little burbling yips escaped from her throat and then she gave up and wept freely, as though she were eight years old again.

Myra gave herself over to anguished sobs, lungs burning for new air. She clutched at her chest in a vain attempt to stem the muscle cramps crushing her rib cage.

She saw the real estate woman in slow motion, running clumsily to her side. Besse's lips were moving with urgent intent but Myra could only hear her own snuffling groans and deafening heartbeat.

She felt the hard push of the taxi driver hurrying her through the French doors and down the front steps. The realtor led the way out, walking backwards and mouthing reassurances that Myra couldn't hear.

The old woman felt the wheelchair touch down solidly at the bottom of the steps, inhaled the cool November air deeply and groaned. Her mouth opened and closed, like a fish on a riverbank. But with each breath, spasms of grief stole away her words. Myra was orphaned and abandoned, alone in the world and yet, a heartbeat later, not alone.

Warmth fell across her left ear, softly tickling her skin with a breathless whisper, a woman's whisper, familiar and gentle and sarcastic.

"Bon appetit."

❦ CHAPTER TWO ❧

Cody Cousins sold his brother's farm on the outskirts of Passable, Mississippi for enough inheritance money to buy anything he wanted, starting with a brand new 1987 Chevy Silverado pickup truck. The dealer quoted him a chokingly high price, but explained the truck was next year's model. Cody slowly did the math and calculated he was getting the truck for a full year for *free*. Sensing the dealer had made a math error in his favor, he quickly ended the negotiations, paid cash and drove off in a Christmas present to himself, one day early.

Cody lived in a rented wooden three-room house six miles outside of town. Termites and wisteria were rapidly pulling the old structure down. He reckoned a shiny new truck would look funny parked in from of such a slum. What he really needed was a good, used mobile home, or better yet, a pull-behind camper.

"You're Upper Crust now, mister Cody," he told himself. Freshly inspired by the thought of buying a trailer, he drove his new truck around Passable with no particular plan or place in mind, keeping an eye peeled for the red-and-white real estate signs.

The best part of house hunting was driving around in the new truck. He loved the power of the Chevy's big engine. It growled like a bear when he pushed the pedal down and the mufflers whined and popped when he downshifted. No sissy automatic transmission on *his* truck, no sir. He wanted the cold smoothness of a clutch under his foot and a gear shifter in his right hand.

Cody headed north up Henderson Hill, partly for the house shopping and partly for the thrill of driving through the tight curve near the top. *"Dead Man's Curve my ass,"* he thought as he built up speed and steered left. Cody had zipped through the curve in his old Ford LTD dozens of times, but today it took him by surprise.

The truck was heavy and didn't corner like he expected. He cut hard to the left and picked his foot up off the gas pedal. Through pure luck, he managed to bring the skid under control and avoid hitting the guardrail.

Howling like a cat, he downshifted and slowed to a more reasonable speed. Now he had a great story to tell at the "Eight Ball" grill, although by the time he got around to telling the tale, the skid would last a lot longer, two wheels would leave the ground, and Cody would survive only because of his vastly superior driving skills.

A half mile farther on, he recognized a "FOR SALE" sign in front of the old Dare place. Beaten-down and overgrown, the yard had seen better days. The house was boxy and strange and not pretty, despite the new paint on its fractured brick.

Cody had heard more than a few stories about that place, disturbing gossip that made little girls cringe. It was said that two people – maybe more – had died in the house. One of 'em was that crazy old Dare woman. Most people said she'd done a suicide, although one or two hinted that she'd been killed by the house itself. In low whispers they'd add that Myra Luckworth had gone plum nuts last month just because she'd gone inside the kitchen, and then they'd nod at each other.

He didn't believe all that prattle, all that ghost talk. Not him, no sir. Cody Cousins didn't get to be sixty-two years old by taking children's stories seriously. There weren't no such things as ghosts.

He had always wondered what the inside of the Dare house looked like. Now he had his chance. And he might even have enough money to buy the old dump if he liked it. That would really be *upper crust.*

Cody parked his truck on the shoulder of the road and got out, shoving the key deep into the pocket of his crisp new jeans where it wouldn't get lost. He paused just long enough to cinch his belt a notch tighter and admire his reflection in the Chevy's big mirrors, noting how a new, white T-shirt made his hair look less gray.

It was a chilly Christmas Eve, an overcast afternoon sky promising rain before dark. He hurried around to the bedroom and peered in the windows, daring to brave the stiffening breeze. His efforts were wasted. There wasn't any furniture to look at and the walls were all painted dull, unimpressive white.

The wind was getting colder but Cody figured that the house owed him one more peek since he had gone to all the trouble of driving way out here. He ran across the brown lawn to the porch, walked up the brick steps and pressed his nose against the glass on the front door. There was a deep hallway on the other side, but again no furniture to look at and the walls were white.

"Big deal!" He didn't know why he thought he might be interested in this house. There wasn't anything special about it. Cody stepped back and looked up at the brick archway surrounding the door. It resembled a big, laughing mouth, tilted up and having a good guffaw at his expense.

The wind blew harder, tiny bits of ice biting his arms and filling him with thoughts of the Chevy's warm cab and the smell of new cloth seats. Standing on the edge of the top step, he made a quick about face and started back to his truck. As Cody shifted his weight, the brick under his left foot popped loose, spinning out from beneath him, leaving him nowhere to go but down.

He hit the bottom step on his hands and knees and bounced, rolling to the ground. Stretched out on the walkway, he stared up at the empty space where the loose brick had once fit. The mortar was still in place, smooth and tight and unbroken, gaping and laughing at him.

His head hurt. He slowly raised himself onto his elbows, then to his knees and finally to his feet. Cody took a few seconds to assess the damage. His left knee was showing through the jeans. It was a bad scrape, but the bleeding would stop soon enough.

His left hand was just plain scary. The middle finger had popped out of its joint and was bent double, forming a blunt question mark sticking out the back. *"That's gonna need a doctor,"* he thought, briefly fantasizing about a nurse admiring his tight new jeans in spite of the torn knee. He tried to straighten out the finger but he couldn't bear to touch it, mostly because of the pain in his other hand. The right wrist was swelling and already turning blue. No doubt about it, there was a broken bone in there somewhere.

Cody limped back to his truck, ready to go home. He stopped when he got to the driver's door, feeling like an idiot. He couldn't drive home... his right hand would never be able to handle a stick shift and his left was too twisted up to steer. Damn, but it was getting cold!

A couple of seconds passed before he had the bright idea to just sit in the truck and get out of the wind. He could always warm up with the engine running, there was no reason to actually *drive* anywhere.

Cody reached out to open the driver's door with his broken wrist and instantly felt the cracked bone grind on itself with a stabbing sensation that shot from his fingers to his elbow. He muttered an angry cuss-word he had learned in the second grade.

When the pain softened enough he tried again, using his left hand this time. Carefully holding the door handle with his dislocated middle finger sticking nearly straight out, Cody winced and grunted and cussed as he lined up both hands on the handle. He took a deep breath, braced himself for the pain to come, then pushed the thumb button and pulled the handle. Nothing happened.

Slowly, dully, Cody Cousins remembered locking the doors. He wanted to cry. The truck key was buried deep in the pocket of his brand new, tight jeans. There was no way he was going to be able to get his busted up hands in there. His only hope was to find someone who would reach into his pants and fish around for the key. He couldn't think of anybody who liked him enough to do that.

Desperate, he looked around the ground for a rock he could use to break the driver's window. He bent over and lifted the stone with his left hand. Being naturally right-handed, Cody managed to throw the rock with all the fury of a preschool girl. The rock struck the window dead center and bounced off.

Needing a larger stone, he agonizingly pried one half the size of a brick from the compacted clay beside the road. Cody threw underhand this time, but the twisted finger wrenched sideways during the toss, making him release early. The heavy stone hit the middle of the door panel and rewarded him with a heartbreaking dent in his brand new truck.

Thirty yards away, the Dare house sat with the front door open, the realtor's padlock hanging by an open shackle. All Cody Cousins would have had to do to get warm was walk inside. He would have found shelter from the rapidly approaching ice storm. Inside, he might have survived, but Cody had completely forgotten the laughing house even existed.

With a shrug, he gave up trying to break into his truck and started walking south down Henderson Road, his thin t-shirt giving him no protection from the blowing sleet, but making his hair seem less gray.

❧ CHAPTER THREE ❧

A single desk lamp glowed in the far corner of the living room, enough light for Jerry to see his typewriter keys without lighting up the whole house. In the distance, an empty log truck fought to survive Dead Man's Curve, downshifting hard and skip-howling with the sudden effort.

Jerry and Nina had learned to ignore the river of sound coursing through the old Dare house. The acoustics were maddening. A whisper in the bedroom echoed in the kitchen, but a shout for help from the stove couldn't be clearly heard beyond the refrigerator.

When the night air turned cool, the walls would pop and thump as oak studs shifted into more comfortable positions. Mice frolicked in an endless attic cotillion, scratching on the other side of the bedroom ceiling with grizzly enthusiasm. At times, something would simply crash to the floor.

Six months earlier, the realtor had glossed over these little annoyances. She was in a hurry to sell the house and an even bigger hurry to leave. It wasn't a perfect place but it was perfectly pleasant and the price was too good to turn down. Nina whispered to Jerry, "It feels like home."

They moved in two days later.

❧❧

Nights like this one made Jerry hate being a writer. He shared the back of his easy chair with a loudly purring bobtail cat, while Nina slept alone in the bedroom, the gentle sound of her breathing broadcast throughout the house. In the hall, an old clock ticked off the seconds and tonked its hammer against a broken chime to mark every hour. In the living room, the story Jerry had been working on since eleven was going nowhere. Blaming the symphony of noise, he pulled the French doors shut and got back to work.

Jerry pushed his imagination as hard as he dared, his tired eyes marrying words into coherent strings of colorful alliteration. Four hours later, he victoriously held up a thin stack of three pages.

Jerry sat back and congratulated himself. *"A pretty good start,"* he thought. He was tired and ready for sleep, but decided to read his Friday opus one last time, basking in the warmth of his own literary fire. Two sentences later, he balled up the pages and tossed them into a wire basket. He was beginning to suspect the story was never actually going to get past the title page.

The black-and-white bobtail readjusted its sleeping position, purring in huffing, rumbling grunts. Out of the corner of his eye, Jerry saw movement in the hallway. He looked up in time to see Nina walk past the French doors, apparently to let the cat out for the night.

But the cat hadn't asked to go out. It was still curled up on the back of the chair, choking on its own purrs. Jerry turned to scratch him and jumped inside his skin when his fingers found the animal gone.

"I guess he did need to go after all," he thought.

He walked to the hallway to tell Nina he would be in bed soon. She hadn't been wearing slippers and the evening was much too cool for bare feet. She should at least have socks on, he thought, pushing on the French doors. They opened with a click, chilling his skin with a sudden inrush of cold air.

Impossibly, Nina wasn't there. The hallway was empty. A sense of strangeness settled over Jerry as he peered into the bedroom and confirmed that Nina was in bed.

"It's late. I'm tired. I'm seeing things." Undeniably, it was his bedtime, too.

Jerry returned to the living room to put away his typewriter. The old bobtail was curled up on the back of the easy chair, softly purring as though nothing had happened.

Nothing at all.

14

❧ CHAPTER FOUR ❧

Some things about husbands defied logic and yoga. Jerry always got up later than Nina, giving her ten minutes for meditation and half an hour for walking. Most days, breakfast was on the table before he was even awake. She didn't understand how he could be such a night person.

The dining room table held him up by the elbows, but his bloodshot eyes weighed him back down. "You look like hell," she told him. "Late night?"

"Later than usual," he groaned, turning a piece of dry toast over in his fingers. "And you?"

"Slept like a baby!" Nina set a plate of eggs mixed with cheese and chopped potatoes onto the table. Jerry helped himself to a large spoonful, pouring the mixture directly onto his toast.

"You were up pretty late, yourself, *baby*," he mocked. "Two in the morning? What were you doing up, anyway?"

She took a bite of dry toast and shook her head in confusion. "What are you talking about?"

"Last night. I saw you. In the hall," he said.

Nina shook her head, "Wasn't me."

"Of course it was you."

"Wasn't me." She hated repeating herself, but this time her objection was subdued. Nina chewed more slowly and wouldn't look at Jerry. Her sudden detachment annoyed him.

"Well, I know what I saw and I saw a *woman* in the hallway! Now last time I checked, it was only you and me living here, so who else did I see last night?"

"OK, suppose it was me. What did I look like?" Nina asked.

"Huh?"

"Describe me," she said. "What was I wearing? What color was my hair?"

Jerry was struck by the strangeness of the question. Her hair was dark brown, of course. He was about to say as much when he remembered seeing her through the glass doors. In the hallway that night her hair hadn't been brown.

"Your hair was *white*," he said. "And it was long, waist length."

Nina turned around and flipped her hair back. Holding it behind her head in one hand, it barely reached her shoulders. "Like I said. Wasn't me."

The hair stood up on the backs of his arms. "I saw *someone*."

"I know," she agreed.

She sat across the table, picking at her eggs but not actually eating anything. Then she locked her eyes onto his and sternly warned him, "Don't laugh."

"OK, I won't."

"And don't call me crazy," Nina held up one finger to reinforce her warning. "I'm not crazy, but I never told you about The Lady because, frankly, I thought maybe I was crazy. Just a little bit. And I think maybe you were crazy a little, too. I think you saw her last night."

"The *lady*. What lady?"

"I don't know," she answered. "Just an old lady. She comes out sometimes."

"Comes out?"

"Comes out, shows up, whatever…"

"You mean I saw a ghost?"

Nina shook her head. "Uh-uh. No such thing as ghosts."

"Well, what then?" he laughed.

Her eyes focused down on her plate. "Don't laugh. Don't. She sort of… she helps me find things."

"What kind of things?"

"Things I've lost. She helps me find stuff I've lost."

"How does she do that?" He tried to stay serious but couldn't hide his amusement.

"You go ahead and laugh, then. She does help. Look, I know this is going to sound crazy, but whenever I lose something real important, the lady shows up and moves something, or knocks something over, and there it is."

"What? There *what* is?"

"Whatever I've been looking for," she groaned. Then her eyes widened and she pointed her fork at him again. "Listen, do you remember that set of emerald earrings you gave me for Christmas about eight years back?"

"Not really."

"Well I do! And they're very special to me," she tilted her head and fluttered her eyelids. "About a month ago, I lost 'em. Couldn't find 'em anywhere, and believe me, I looked *everywhere*. I spent hours combing through this old house and those earrings just weren't here."

"And?"

"And one night about two weeks back – must've been three in the morning – I heard a loud *'thump'* in the hallway and I got out of bed to see what it was. It was my purse. Somehow, it had fallen off the chair onto the floor. When I picked it up, right there underneath it on the floor, there were my earrings!"

Jerry leaned back and smiled patronizingly. "So, let me see if I understand where you're going with this," he started. "You put your earrings in your purse, got all upset when you couldn't find them, and then one night the cat knocked over your purse…"

"Oh, I just *knew* you wouldn't understand." Nina dropped her fork into the middle of her plate, picked up the dishes from her side of the table and headed for the kitchen. What was left of her breakfast went into the garbage and the plate went into the sink, loudly.

Jerry persisted, "You just can't be serious about this old lady, this *ghost*."

"I didn't say she was a ghost, now did I?"

"No, you didn't, but you sure told a good ghost story."

"You saw her last night. Did she seem real to you then?"

Jerry didn't answer.

"This morning, when I got up, I bumped into the hallway armoire," she said. "One of the drawers was open. Look what was inside." Nina held out her arm and showed Jerry an old Timex wristwatch.

Jerry squinted at the black plastic treasure. "Oh boy. A fifteen-dollar watch."

Nina explained. "It is not. This is a real, red LED ladies' Timex."

"What's wrong with it?"

"Nothing. I lost it two or three weeks ago. It's collectors' item. I thought it was lost for good." She shrugged and admired her watch again. "Then, last night, you saw The Lady."

"And this morning, you found your watch." They sat in mutual silence and listened to the hallway clock tick. "So now, what? You believe in ghosts?"

"Not particularly. Do you?"

"Not at all," he said.

"And yet you watched her walk down the hallway."

"I still think it could have been you. Maybe you were sleepwalking. Maybe…"

She interrupted him. "I've seen her three or four times. One time she was in the living room and I was in the hallway. All the other times, she was in the hallway and I was in the living room."

"Your point?"

"You had the living room doors closed last night, didn't you?"

"How did you know that?"

"Every time I've ever seen her, The Lady was on the other side of those glass doors. I have a theory. I think you have to be looking through the glass in order to see her."

Jerry finished his breakfast, which had cooled a bit during the discussion. He thought about the four or five times he had sat up late and was startled by a sudden silence in the house. Four or five times, he thought he had seen Nina looking in on him, peering at him through the French doors.

NO, dammit! It was Nina behind the door, not some old dead lady.

And yet, clearly it was not quite Nina.

✐ CHAPTER FIVE ✐

The incident with The Lady was was simply covered over with silence. This was better than arguing about something silly like ghosts.

Nina and Jerry rarely fought, a remarkable achievement considering they had been married nearly twenty years. Jerry had a handful of cute theories that explained why they got along so well. Nina simply blamed everything bad on the cat.

Born bereft of a tail, Kat was rescued from a life of chasing rats around the barn and given free run of the Dare house. Once during his first year, he found himself the center of attention while carrying a shiny person-thing into his lair for closer examination. Nina caught him *in flagrante delicto*, goose-stepping down the hallway with one of her gold chains dangling out either side of his thieving, guilty jaws.

It was the only time in Kat's memory that he had ever put a person-thing into his mouth, except once on Christmas morning and maybe one other time.

From that day on, Kat was openly blamed every time one of the persons lost something, and he didn't appreciate the way they looked at him. He went under the bed, shoving a shoe aside with his shoulder, and vanished into a dark corner. It was hiding time.

"I'm going to stop giving you jewelry," Jerry threatened.

"You didn't give it to me. I *earned* it." She was feeling the angry edge of panic. Nina was meeting her mother for lunch tomorrow afternoon and her mother would be wearing her gold Phi Beta Kappa key. It was one of the few things they had in common.

Somehow, Nina's key had slipped from its slender chain. And now it was gone.

"I'll bet that darn cat of yours got it."

"Well, give him this much credit, the little guy has good taste."

Nina scooped all the loose jewelry and chains from the bottom of her organizer and piled the mess on the mattress. Jerry got down on his hands and knees and looked under the bed. Kat zipped past him, loudly protesting the intrusion.

"Did you look in the bottom of your jewelry box?" Jerry suggested.

"Of course."

"Did you look in the bottom of your purse?" His voice betrayed no concern whatsoever.

"Yes, of *course* I did." Nina hated this part of losing things. Jerry pretended to help, acting as if he really cared about her trinkets. That's all a Phi Beta Kappa key was to him anyway – a silly little gold trinket – but then he didn't have one. Next, he'd ask about the dirty clothes hamper, and then the bathroom, and then the Incredible Mister Stupid question.

"Did you look in the hamper?" Without waiting for her answer, he followed with, "How about the bathroom? Did you look there?"

Nina kept her back to him, squeezed her eyes shut and recited The Wife's Prayer out loud. *"Dear God, please make my husband go away."*

"So, when was the last time you saw your little key?" There it was, the Incredible Mister Stupid question right on time.

"If," she paused to let the word take root, *"If* I could remember *that,* then I wouldn't be doing *this!"* She gestured at the knotted pile of shiny bracelets and tangled chains in the middle of the bed. It was going to take an hour or more to separate some of this mess, but there was a chance the little gold key was buried somewhere inside.

Kat landed on the corner of the bed with an intentionally innocent expression and headed straight for the pile of tangled toys. "OFF!" Nina ordered, pointing at the door. Sensing the nearness of his demise, Kat decided to find toys elsewhere.

Nina put the Gordian knot of chains and pendants into a box and spent the next two hours sitting on the couch, carefully pulling them apart. Jerry made adjustments to the television antenna, slowly perfecting the salt-and-pepper image so they could watch "Cheers" and spend another fine evening at home doing nothing at all. They both fell asleep before midnight without bothering to leave the couch.

Tonight, the bed belonged entirely to a fat bobtail. He tested the pillows and settled in to a vivid dream of running, twisting and accelerating, inches ahead of a vicious dog's snapping jaws. This was Kat's Happy Dream, one of his favorites.

In the living room, Jerry slept lightly, barely touching the edge of dream-sleep. His mind was busy typing a new story and his shoulder ached from the weight of Nina's head. From the way her hands twitched, she was dreaming about pulling chains apart.

A crash of metal jerked her instantly awake. Something in the hallway had fallen. Sleeping on the couch had given her a crick and she twisted her neck to relieve the pain. Jerry was already on his feet, crouched, looking intently at the hallway. She turned her head in the direction he was facing and froze.

They both stared straight at the woman on the other side of the French doors. She was small and barefoot, with white hair dangling down to her waist. Wearing a light robe and a shawl, she moved effortlessly from the bedroom to the front door, pausing to turn toward Nina and smile. Then she shimmered, and then she simply wasn't there any more.

Nobody dared breathe. The only sound in the room was the ticking of the wall clock. Jerry had sweat on his upper lip.

"KEYS!" Nina splintered the silence, pushing Jerry's heart closer to full arrest.

"Jeez God, woman!" he cursed. "What's wrong with you?"

"Look in the hallway. I heard *keys* hit the floor. I'm sure of it. Go look!"

"I'm not going out there." Jerry shook his head.

"Oh, for crying out loud, you coward! She's already gone. Just go look!"

"*You* look."

Nina groaned and walked out into the hall, holding her neck to stifle the pain from sleeping on his shoulder. Her key chain lay on the tile floor, having apparently fallen from the dish above the piano keyboard. She bent over to pick it up.

A glint of silvery yellow from beneath the piano caught her eye. Curious, she reached underneath with her fingers and brushed the shiny object out onto the floor.

"What is it?" Jerry asked.

"My key," she answered. "My little Phi Beta Kappa key. I knew she'd help." Nina held the key in front of her face to admire it and walked into the bedroom to put it away and get some real sleep.

"Jerry, come get this cat off the bed, please."

❧ CHAPTER SIX ❧

The universe was spinning slightly off-axis. It was Friday, a day early for their weekly drive into Passable for groceries. Jerry asked Nina whether she wanted to talk.

"Oh, I don't like the way this conversation is going, already. It's about The Lady, isn't it?"

"Just one question," he reached over and turned the volume down on the radio. "Did we see a ghost last night?"

"I don't believe in ghosts and I know you don't, either. You've told me that yourself."

"Well, then, what did you see last night?"

"The same thing you did, Jer."

He had to make sure. "White hair, flowing gown, bare feet?"

"She seems to be nice," Nina said. "I kind of like having her around."

"A ghost? You want to live in a haunted house?"

"I didn't say she was a ghost. I was just saying that I wasn't afraid of her. I wonder who she is."

"*Was*," Jerry corrected. "She's dead."

"If you believe in ghosts. I'd still like to find out who she is…was."

"How do we do that?"

"Simple. We ask somebody."

"Oh, we're gonna be real popular around Passable."

"It'll be easier than you think," she said. Nina pointed at a dirt driveway off to their right. "Pull in here. I'm going to ask Suzin."

Jerry braked hard and turned in, skidding lightly as his wheels touched gravel and locked up. The scraping noise could be heard inside Passable Beauty, the only beauty shop in the Henderson Hill neighborhood. None of the customers ever called it by its name, though. To them, it was just "Suzin's".

"Let me do the talking, sweetie," Nina warned as she got out of the car.

Suzin Scott had married well. Her husband was steadfast and predictable, and had been easily badgered into building the beauty shop. Barely large enough to hold one working chair, the tiny emporium had the dual amenities of air conditioning and gossip. Suzin's turned into *the* gathering place of local women, a quiet hub of feminine conversation and conditioning.

Jerry followed Nina through Suzin's door with the boldness of a man who didn't know what he was doing. A few women were already inside, leaving barely enough room to turn around.

"Hello, Sooz," Nina said. "Got time to trim my bangs?"

"Sure, hon! You're next. Find a place to sit and I'll be finished with Margaret in a moment."

Jerry looked on in amused horror as a reclining body, face-up and faceless with only a mass of towels for a head, slowly lifted one fish-white arm toward the sky. From within the terry cloth mound Margaret's muffled voice called out, "Hi, Nina."

"Hi ya, Marge," Nina looked around the tiny room and discovered a folding chair leaning against the wall outside the bathroom. She opened it in the corner nearest to the front door and sat down on half the seat. She looked up at Jerry and patted the empty half of the chair.

"Thanks, I'll just go wait in the car."

"Oh, don't be that way," she mocked. "You can put up with a few minutes of girl talk while I get my hair scissored."

The other customers smiled nervously and fidgeted. A man in their private fortress was something they could not readily accept. Nina continued in the great Southern tradition of asking about the health of every family member whose name she could remember. "How's Ralph doin', Sooz?"

"Oh, he cain't complain," Suzin drawled.

"He does, though," added a giggling voice from the opposite corner.

"Hi, Caroline," Nina greeted her with a finger wave. "I didn't see you there."

Practically speaking, it was unlikely she had overlooked Caroline Wilkins, a Choctaw woman who was large even by tribal standards. Caroline had married a white man some years earlier, moved off the Pearl River reservation and made her home in Passable.

Jerry stood by the door saying nothing, lost in thought. The feminine chatter passed by him without actually being heard, until Nina broke the pattern.

"Say, girls," she began, "I found an old photograph in the kitchen drawer the other day."

"Oh, that's a lovely kitchen," said Brancy Wright, sitting next to Nina. "I walked through that old house when it went up for sale."

Nina had heard this from everyone she knew. They had all walked through the house, or peered into its windows. Everybody loved it. But nobody bought it.

"Yes, I was sort of surprised that this snapshot was left behind," she told Brancy. "Funny old photo. It's a picture of a woman standing in front of our house. I wondered if anybody knew who she might be."

Suzin chimed in, "There ain't been many people living in that old house, honey. Why don't you bring that old photo 'round and we'll take a look."

"Yeah, it's kinda hard to tell who she is without actually seeing the picture. If you're gonna be home later, I'll stop by and look at it," Brancy said.

"Oh, it's not important. I was just wondering who she was," Nina brushed off the offer. Her bluff had failed.

Jerry motioned for them to leave. "Come on, Nina. I got that *thing* downtown in a half hour."

Nina said her goodbyes and offered Suzin a rain check for the trim. Jerry crunched across the gravel to their car slightly ahead of her. When they opened their doors, a pale woman in her late sixties walked up. There was something starkly odd about her.

She was neatly dressed in plain white, with a white shawl pulled close around her shoulders. Her eyes, Nina noticed, were the color of granite. She didn't remember seeing her in Suzin's, but she hadn't really been paying that much attention. The stranger extended a thin hand and introduced herself.

"Hello, my name is Charlotte Montgomery."

"A pleasure to meet you," Nina replied. As she shook the old, fragile hand, she could see the details of the bones in her fingers, almost as though the skin had turned transparent. Her feet, surprisingly, were bare.

"The lady in your photograph, may I ask, what did she look like?" There was cultured southern lilt to her accent, softly bending her words without a twang.

"Well, she was about your height, with waist-length hair. White hair, I believe." Nina turned to Jerry. "Isn't that right, sweetie?"

"Uh huh," he agreed.

Charlotte Montgomery stood at attention, her hands crossed in front of her waist. She cleared her throat and spoke in a voice as soft as lilac.

"I know the girl you're looking for. Her name was Abigail Dare."

❦ CHAPTER SEVEN ❧

"Tomatoes were a hard crop, but those were hard times."
Charlotte Montgomery

Orvis Dare was a God-fearing man, a man who listened when the Bible was read to him. He knew his Maker had a plan for him the day he met his son, who he named William, after his own father. Billy would grow up to be a farmer, just like Orvis.

In 1920, farming was about the only way to make a living in Passable County. The bank was delighted to loan Orvis the money he needed to buy a hundred acres off the Chunky River and start a farm. By 1928, Orvis had a tractor, a new Chevrolet pickup truck and a mule. A year later, everything changed forever.

Farms fell to the mortgage axe by the hundreds. The bank in Passable presented Orvis Dare an eviction notice with an order to surrender all personal property. They attached a hand-written list of every item they wanted turned over before Orvis left the premises.

He packed up his belongings that night and left the farm in a mule-drawn wagon, his wife, Rowena, at his side, stoic and unmoved by the cards Fate had dealt her.

"The bank will eventually require the safe return of this here mule," she observed.

"That is unlikely, Rowena. The mule was not on the bank's list of property they expected us to give back."

She turned and took notice of a folded tent laid over the top of their pots and pans. "And the oilcloth? I distinctly remember seeing the camp tent on their list."

"It won't hurt them any to ask for the tent twice."

Orvis Dare never told a soul he lost everything during the Great Depression because he didn't believe it. He had his hands and his wife and young Billy, and people were happy to pay him for odd jobs. They survived every day, not in comfort, but as a family. Had the economic circumstances been even the slightest bit different, Orvis would not have knocked on Harrison Quimby's door.

All anybody knew about Quimby was that he was old, he lived on some sort of pension, and he sounded British. Most people thought he came from Australia or England. He didn't talk about himself and people around Passable didn't pry.

Asking for work door-to-door was humbling, but Orvis had no other way to feed his family. He told Quimby he was temporarily "between abodes" and offered to work in exchange for a few days' shelter for his wife and child. For himself, he asked nothing.

Quimby handed over the keys to a hunting cabin he kept outside of Passable. "Use it as long as you need it," he said. "There are canned goods in the cabinet that will no doubt spoil if not eaten."

Unable to believe the generosity of the offer, Orvis asked why he would do such a thing. Here he stood, a stranger to this old man. He had expected to be treated with suspicion.

Quimby simply answered, "Sometimes you hear a whisper in your ear and you have to obey." Orvis understood. He heard this whisper the day Billy was born.

Harrison Quimby died in his sleep the following year. He had no heirs but he owned his land outright, so it was a few years before Passable County called the taxes delinquent and sold his house and property at auction. No one took notice of a small hunting cabin hidden away on a back road, surrounded by an acre of tomatoes ripening on the vine.

In the spring of 1932, Rowena Dare took ill with typhus. William helped Orvis bury her beside the cabin. All they had left was each other, an old mule and the good ground they worked together. It wasn't much and it wasn't easy, but Orvis and his eleven-year old son made do with what they had.

Every Saturday during the growing season they'd hitch up their mule, load a cart with cheap woven baskets full of fresh tomatoes and roll out of Passable. Ten miles away, State Road 17 was the closest asphalt highway with a shoulder wide enough to allow cars to pull over and transact business.

Getting to the tomato stand took the better part of a day by mule cart, its wood and iron wheels finding every rut and twist on the hard packed road. More than once, a weak spoke splintered, stranding them in the hot sun. Billy would ride the mule back home and get tools while Orvis stayed with the wagon to keep the possums from eating all their profits.

It was a hard way to live, harder than most boys would endure. Billy turned fourteen and grew up completely in 1934, the year the wagon broke its singletree a few miles short of the stand. He rode the mule back home and returned with a satchel of tools just after dark, but by then the July sun had taken his daddy and the crows had ruined the crop.

He couldn't move Orvis' body by himself and he wouldn't leave it for the coyotes, so Billy got back on the mule and set out to find help. The nearest house was Hyram Northbridge's place, five miles back in the direction he had just come. Riding at a slow, deliberate pace in the darkness, they ambled into Hyram Northbridge's yard shortly after nine.

The mule announced their arrival with a bray, startling Hyram out of his reading chair. Mrs. Northbridge was in the kitchen with her almost-twelve-year old daughter, wiping the last dinner plates clean.

The ladies remained in the house while Hyram sorted out the reason for this late-night intrusion. From the kitchen window, Mrs. Northbridge watched as the young boy who sometimes delivered tomatoes wheeled his mule around and disappeared back into the dark at a slow trot.

Hyram grabbed his hat and a shovel and kissed his wife on the cheek as he hurried out the door. "Don't wait up, I'll be late," he warned, loading the shovel into the trunk of his Buick.

"What's wrong?" Mrs. Northbridge asked. "Wasn't that the tomato boy?"

"Billy Dare, yes," Hyram answered. "I have to go help him. His father died tonight and his body's still laid out on the road."

"Why do *you* have to go?"

"Because I *can*," he answered.

She returned to the dishes, wondering how such a young boy would get along without any family. It occurred to her that he wasn't much older than her own daughter, but at least she knew where Abigail would live if she were suddenly orphaned. She had no idea where Billy Dare called "home".

Hyram and Billy unloaded the wagon and manhandled Orvis' mortal remains into the back. Illuminated by the Buick's headlights, they repaired the singletree and hitched the reluctant mule to the wagon. Billy followed the car as far as the Northbridge driveway, assured Hyram he'd be all right in the dark, and waved goodbye. The following morning, he dug a hole nearly as deep as he was tall and buried Orvis next to Rowena.

The tomato season still had two good pickings left in it. The little bit of tomato money Billy earned went further than before. He was careful and spent as little as possible. Winter was coming and Billy had to survive until the first harvest in May. He was really too young to tend the vines by himself, but he didn't know how to do anything else so he grew tomatoes.

꙼ꙮꙨ

Two years later, a week before Christmas, a man named Kennison Meeder knocked on the cabin's front door. Kennison had a reputation for rudeness, although he preferred to think of himself as assertive.

"Tell yer parents to come out and talk to me," he told Billy between puffs and bites on an old, smoldering cigar.

"They cain't," Billy said curtly. "What d'you want?"

"What I want, boy, is to speak with yer father, and if he ain't at home then I'll speak with yer mother. Now! I ain't got the time to dilly-dally with no teenager."

Billy said, "All right. Follow me. They're 'round back."

Kennison smiled inside. Chomping on a cigar always had this effect on the feeble-minded. He was busy examining the outside of the cabin. Clean and well maintained, it needed paint.

"Here they are," Billy announced. He pointed to Rowena's grave first and said, "This is my mother and this one over here is my father. As I told you inside, they cain't come to the door.

"I'm terribly sorry," Kennison apologized. "How did they... I mean, when?" he stammered.

"It's all right," Billy said. "I buried my mother a little over three years ago, and my dad passed the year after that."

Kennison Meeder asked questions, short and easy ones at first. Billy opened up immediately, answering openly and then volunteering opinions, plans, and his outlook on life. Kennison wanted to know about the tomato vines. Billy gave him a short course on growing, selling, and cooking tomatoes.

Billy finally had a question of his own. "Who are you?"

Kennison gave him his name, again, and told Billy he lived in Irondale.

"That didn't answer my question," Billy told him brazenly.

Kennison said he was looking for good spots to hunt deer and he was hoping to get the landowner's permission. He left out the fact that he had bought the land from the county a year earlier and had come down to investigate rumors of a squatter on his land.

Instead he took Billy on as an apprentice bricklayer. The boy had a good eye and quick hands and before long, he trusted Billy with easy tasks, letting him build steps and repoint old veneer without supervision.

Working for Kennison Meeder meant doing a lot of travel, but the pay was good. The road between Passable and Irondale was still dirt, but more and more cars were using it and there was talk the county supervisor was going to get money from Jackson to lay asphalt between the two towns.

Billy saved up as much of his pay as he could for nearly a year and bought Mr. Meeder's four-year old Chevy pickup truck for two hundred dollars. Billy didn't have all the money, but Kennison was ready to trust him and advanced him seventy-five dollars on his pay.

In early May 1939, Mr. Meeder sent him out to the Northbridge place to build a brick stairway up to their porch. The wooden steps Hyram Northbridge had built and repaired and patched and fixed had finally given in to years of relentless Mississippi rain-to-sun-to-rain. Mrs. Northbridge could tolerate creaking, but when she heard snapping and felt the stairs move ever so slightly sideways, she reached deep into her savings and bought a set of brick steps for Mr. Northbridge's birthday, still two weeks away.

Hyram Northbridge knew nothing about his wife's plans. He met Billy in the driveway and stopped him from getting out of the truck, quizzing him about the load of bricks in the cargo bed. Billy didn't know the stairs were to be a birthday surprise and he wasted no time spilling the beans. When Hyram found out his wife had spent all her egg money, he protested at the top of his lungs, simultaneously pointing out the exact place he wanted his new steps.

The screen door squeaked open. Hyram and Billy looked up at the same moment. Abigail was sixteen and when she saw Billy, all she could do was stare. Hyram didn't like the look in his daughter's eyes and decided to get old Kennison to come out in person and finish the stairs, but it was too late. Billy had taken notice of The Daughter and was no longer actively listening to The Father.

Hyram laughed, "From the look on your face, you'd think you hadn't never seen Abbie before."

Billy turned back toward Hyram. "That's little Abigail? I guess I just never noticed her 'til now."

"Well, you haven't been out here since your dad died. I guess there's a difference between a girl who's twelve and one that's sixteen," Hyram laughed.

Billy didn't answer. He couldn't stop himself from staring at Abbie.

Hyram saw the two of them gaping at each other and gave up. "I guess you better get to work on them steps, son." Billy didn't hear him. "Billy! *Steps.*"

"Oh...yessir." Billy got out of the truck and set to work unloading brick and bags of mortar and buckets and tools. By the time he was done ripping out the old stair steps, it was nearly noon.

Abigail couldn't believe how horribly her day was going. That tomato wagon boy from when she was just a little girl was standing *right there* and now she was nearly grown up and too scared to move. All she could do was squeak and grin like she was a little girl again.

Mrs. Northbridge walked up behind her daughter and handed her two glasses of water. "Take our visitor something to drink," she instructed.

Abigail took the glasses and asked, "Two glasses?"

"Don't be rude. Sit and keep him company until he's finished and then bring the glasses back inside," her mother said.

The girl blushed with fear. "Mama...no! What will I say?"

"Say 'hello'," Mrs. Northbridge advised. "And act like a lady." With that final admonition, she held the squeaking screen door open and ushered her daughter out onto the porch.

◆ CHAPTER EIGHT ◆

"Whirlwinds come at you fast and carry you away before you have a chance to fight."
Charlotte Montgomery

"How strange," Billy muttered.

He had come out to the Northbridge house late Friday afternoon to check up on the handrail he had added to the porch steps. It wasn't the first time he had inspected his stairs. In the past month, he had found a reason to stop by nearly every Friday or Saturday, always fussing over every chip and scuff.

The week before, he brought some short lengths of iron pipe and fashioned a sturdy handrail. Mrs. Northbridge kept him company throughout the project, asking all sorts of questions having nothing to do with bricklaying – how are you getting along, is Mr. Meeder paying you enough, do you still have the mule?

Billy caught himself glancing up at the screen door, hoping for a glimpse of the pretty girl who occasionally peeked through at him. Mrs. Northbridge kept bringing his thoughts back to the work he was doing, and when it was done she offered Billy a few dollar bills from her pocket. Of course, he declined and, of course, she insisted, so Billy promised her he would accept payment only after his work had set for a week and passed his own inspection.

The Northbridge house was the only job he had ever subjected to such scrutiny. Seven days after installing the handrail and true to his word, Billy showed up for the inspection. He was astonished to find that a brick had broken loose. A close examination of the mortar revealed a series of smooth, straight cuts around the empty corner. "That's really strange," he repeated.

"What's strange?" Abbie's voice startled him. He turned his head slightly and saw two shoeless, filthy feet standing less than a yard away.

"The brick. It looks like it's been... I don't know," he shook head in disbelief. "These looks like *cut* marks."

"Maybe somebody broke the old brick off," she offered. "Let me see."

She knelt closer to study the missing brick. Billy inhaled through his nose and came alive inside when he realized the perfume attached to those two muddy feet had been recently applied for his benefit. He wondered whether Mrs. Northbridge had given her daughter permission to dab.

"Looks like someone used a tool. Maybe a knife, or a, oh, I don't know. What do you call a tool like this?" she asked, holding out a small wood chisel. Its cutting edge was dull and chinked, completely ruined, almost as if it had been used on a rock, or...

"Oh, Abbie," Billy groaned. "Your daddy's gonna be mighty upset if he finds out." He reached out and took it from her hand, his fingertips brushing her upturned palm. He would always remember the first time he touched her.

She pulled a cane-bottom chair over to the steps and watched Billy scrape the damaged mortar and reset the missing brick. He wiped his hands on an old rag to signal he was finished.

"Is that all there is to it?" Abigail asked. "Kind of hard to believe that you make money just for doin' that."

Mrs. Northbridge pushed the screen door open with the toe of her shoe and produced two glasses of sweet tea. "Abbie, would you please take one of these to your guest?"

"Yes, ma'am," her daughter replied, passing the cool drink to Billy. She wrapped her fingers around it making it impossible for him to take it without touching her hand to steady the glass. When he did, she pressed her hand almost imperceptibly against his and let it dwell. He immediately saw through her ploy, nervously disguising his delight.

"There's one for you, too," Mrs. Northbridge reminded the girl. "You can sit out here for awhile and watch the brick set." She pulled a dollar from her apron pocket and held it out for Billy.

He shook his head and tried to decline payment. "I take care of my work," he said. "These here stairs are still under my guarantee."

"Please take the money, William," she insisted. "You've been more than diligent about these steps and you haven't asked for a thing." She pressed the dollar into his hand, smiled and gently added, "Besides, I wouldn't want you to think that we Northbridge women were a pack of *chiselers*."

Mrs. Northbridge then turned to Abigail and said, "In the course of your conversations with Mr. Dare, you might steer the topic in the direction of dinner."

Abigail just stared at her mother. Mrs. Northbridge leaned closer and whispered, "Invite him to stay for dinner." Then she vanished through the screen door, leaving the task of hospitality to her daughter. Abigail fidgeted with her glass and then blurted out what seemed to be some sort of invitation.

"Mama wants you to stay for dinner," she announced. Her eyes shifted toward Billy, looking for an answer.

"What about you?" he asked.

"Oh, I'm having dinner, too."

Billy rinsed his hands and tools under the cool flow from the garden hose. "Then, kindly tell your mother that I accept her invitation."

"William Dare!" she snapped, "*I'm* the one inviting you."

"Actually, you said your mama wanted me to stay for dinner. Maybe I should ask HER to go for a ride in my truck."

"A ride?" she asked with renewed interest. Abigail followed him out onto the driveway.

"Sure. Tomorrow. Over to Passable Lake," he said as he piled his tools into the open bed of the truck. "Oh, you can go too. There's plenty of room back here."

Mrs. Northbridge leaned out the front door and called, "Dinner's on the table, kids!"

Abbie walked beside him, escorting Billy back to the house. Without looking at him, she said, "Mama's too old for you."

"Maybe so, maybe so," he agreed. "She's very nice, though...Unghh!" His lungs huffed out when Abbie tagged his ribs with a playful elbow. Billy stopped walking and took on a more serious tone. "Okay, then, how 'bout you? Are you too old for me, too?"

"Nooo, I'd say I'm just about right."

The screen door creaked open and Mrs. Northbridge came all the way out onto the porch, her fists sternly planted on her hips. "William, we have rules about dinner. If you're not at the table in fifteen seconds, your plate will be given to the dogs."

"Mrs. Northbridge, you don't have dogs."

Abbie gasped. "No, Billy. She means *wild* dogs! Hurry inside before she whistles 'em up!" She pushed Billy into the house, laughing and promising herself that she'd never forget how delightful it felt to touch his back.

At dinner, Mr. Northbridge wanted to know as much as possible about brickwork. Mr. Dare was only too happy to oblige, providing details and anecdotes Mr. Northbridge found highly entertaining. Mrs. Northbridge wanted to know about Billy's girlfriends, and noticed the well-hidden delight in her daughter's eyes when she saw him blush and admit to having been too busy for courtship.

Mr. Northbridge asked about his schooling, to his immediate regret. Billy hadn't had any formal learning, but his mother taught him to read and write, and she borrowed a schoolbook and used it to teach him to add and subtract. After she died, he learned about tomato farming from his father and about brickwork from Mr. Meeder.

Mrs. Northbridge inquired about his future plans. Billy told her he had a repair job scheduled for Wednesday next and he was supposed to start learning how to build brick arches as soon as Mr. Meeder got a customer who needed a brick arch.

He chuckled as he remembered an amusing repointing job he had recently finished. "The customer was a big Polish guy. For the life of me, I couldn't tell you their name…it's impossible to pronounce. Kinda like holding a mouthful of marbles and saying 'Monongahela' backwards!"

Hyram didn't laugh. "Germany invaded Poland last week, son. This Polish family with the funny name no longer has a home. Except for Passable."

"I don't follow politics too closely," Billy said, "but I feet pretty safe with Germany all the way over on the other side of the ocean."

"Hitler's got U-boats. That ocean ain't as big as you think."

The chitchat had bled out of the conversation. Only the sounds of silverware, water glasses, and chewing could be heard for five long seconds.

Abigail broke the silence. "Billy's taking me down to Passable Lake tomorrow."

"Oh?" Hyram looked up from his plate and studied the young man's face. "Is that so?"

"Well, uh, I, uh…" he stammered, "I asked her… Abbie… Abigail… your daughter…"

Abigail's mother interrupted the tension. "Well, I think that's just fine. I'll have some sandwiches ready for you to take along," she said.

Dinner was over too soon. Billy thanked Mrs. Northbridge for the fine meal, and shook Mr. Northbridge's hand as he was shown to the porch. Abigail pushed around her father and waved at Billy through the screen door.

"See you tomorrow," she said, wishing she could think of something else to say that would keep him on her porch for another hour.

"Twelve-thirty," Billy said.

"One-thirty," Hyram corrected. He wanted to make sure Billy Dare knew who was in charge of things around the Northbridge house.

ᔍ CHAPTER NINE ᔌ

"Abbie was a force of nature, gentle and overpowering."
Charlotte Montgomery

Billy sat in the driver's seat of his pickup truck with the engine turned off, staring at Abbie in the quiet darkness of early December. Her face startlingly lighted by the soft glow from the kitchen window, he saw her as though for the first time. She was taller, now, and not so thin, with a sharper jaw line and darker eyes. He wondered why he couldn't remember the exact date when she became a woman.

Tonight, he was planning on telling her how he felt about things. Not things you can buy or carry around in a pocket, but things that a man is reluctant to discuss with a girl – a woman – who means so much to his continued existence. He would tell her soon, but he was pretty sure she already knew how he felt.

Abbie interlaced her fingers with his and squeezed. She had turned seventeen officially an hour earlier over a dessert of chocolate cake and sweet tea, excusing Billy and herself from the table without finishing the last forkful from her plate, a sign that her state of mind had taken a moody turn.

She squeezed his hand again, a quick, hard pump, a prelude to something important. She started to speak but held back with a heavy sigh. Billy waited patiently through two more false starts before deciding to finally tell Abigail Northbridge everything that was on his mind. He took a breath and opened his mouth to speak her name.

Before he could utter a word, she released her grip and blood once again pumped into his fingers. "I'm not going to wait for you say it first," she said. "I'm supposed to wait. That's what ladies do. But I'm not going to. I'm in love with you, Billy."

Her eyes sought out his, and her hand caressed his shoulder.

"I'm not sure what to say," he said. "I'm glad you told me before I ran off with someone else."

"Don't be flippant, William Dare!" She slapped the back of his head with her caressing hand.

"Sorry."

"Sorry won't do. I'm in love with you and you're going to marry me. Don't tell me you haven't had thoughts on the subject."

"Well, I…"

"I expect a proposal and an engagement ring, of course…"

"…of course…"

"…but first, you'll have to ask Daddy's permission. I'll want children. Five is a good number. We'll name the first boy after you."

Billy listened for nearly ten minutes as Abbie reviewed her upcoming nuptials and their subsequent life together – where they would live; how much savings he would need; which church they would attend (hers); drinking (never); smoking (never); gambling and other vile habits (never).

Abruptly, she stopped talking. Billy stared at this breathtaking, breathless girl next to him and realized he was a mere rabbit when she was near… lured, trapped and skinned. "Are you done?" he asked.

"I think so," she answered. Then she gave a quick little laugh. "I'm sorry I was so long-winded," she said. "I just had to get all that off my chest."

"Okay," He frowned, thinking hard of what he would say, or do, next.

"I love you," she said tentatively. After a short silence from him, she tried again. "Billy, I love you." His eyes stayed serious and he didn't answer. "Don't you have anything to say to *me*?"

"No," he stated flatly, jerking the driver's door open. Without looking back, he charged through the Northbridge's front yard and up the porch steps.

Abbie hurried to get her door open and chased after him, demanding that he stop and talk to her.

Billy ignored his pursuer and marched into the house, letting the screen door slam shut before she could catch it. Hyram Northbridge looked up from his reading chair to see who had barged in so rudely.

"Mr. Northbridge, we have to talk." He turned toward Mrs. Northbridge who was standing in the kitchen, wiping a dinner plate. "Excuse me, ma'am, but I need to talk to your husband in private, please."

"Of course, Billy." She snagged Abigail by one arm and pulled her backwards out onto the porch, closing the front door behind them so the men could have some privacy.

Billy waited until he heard the screen door close, then turned toward Hyram. "Mister Northbridge," he paused to select the words he would use next. He stood at attention and tried again. "Sir…"

"Get on with it."

"Sir, Abigail and me have to get married." Billy grinned, satisfied that he had said what was on his mind.

Hyram's expression changed. Billy tried to figure out what the pinched eyebrows meant. He thought about it and then realized his mistake.

"Oh… I mean Abigail and *I* have to get married. Sorry."

Hyram slowly rose to his feet, clenching and unclenching his fists. "What? What did you say?"

This wasn't the reaction Billy expected. He tried changing the sentence. "I have to marry your daughter?"

Hyram's face twisted slightly. Billy decided to explain why he was asking for Abbie's hand. "Mister Northbridge, don't misunderstand. I don't really *want* to get married, but your daughter won't leave me alone. She said she wants five kids...FIVE. Oh, and I don't make enough money. I really don't know what to do. If I marry her, I'll never have any peace. If I don't marry her... well, sir, that's just silly, isn't it? I'm lost here. Isn't there a compromise or something? Maybe I ought to just go ahead and marry her. It'd be easier that way."

Hyram expression softened and his hands loosened. He cleared his throat and said, "I'm terribly sorry, William. I have to agree with you. Just go ahead and get married. I don't see that you have any other option."

Billy shrugged. "Could be worse, I suppose. At least she's pretty."

"Well, it's good to have a positive outlook regarding these matters." He put a hand on Billy's shoulder and guided him toward the front door. "Having skill as a bricklayer is important, no doubt. It'll make sure you have food on the table. But a sense of humor can save your life."

"Yes, sir."

"Seriously, Bill. Do you love her? Do you love my daughter?"

Billy carefully weighed his answer. "Yes, sir. I do."

"Have you told *her* that?"

"Uh, no, not in so many words. It was never the right time. I'm sure she knows. Well, I just sort of assumed..."

"You assumed...oh, poor William!" Hyram slapped Billy on the back and laughed.

He opened the front door and guided him out onto the porch, where the women waited impatiently. They jumped to their feet, surprised and confused by the sudden appearance of the men after so short a conversation.

Hyram broke the silence, grinning. "Good news, Missus Northbridge! We're finally gettin' rid of Abbie."

✎ CHAPTER TEN ✎

"The whole world seemed to waiting for the starting gun, but all lined up in a circle, facing the middle."
                                    Charlotte Montgomery

The next morning, Hyram asked, "Where are the two of you going to live?"

The cabin. It was clean and neat, but it was still little more than a kitchen with two rooms and a roof. No matter how much Billy would have preferred to own a nice house, there was no avoiding the obvious. He was going to take Hyram's daughter away and move into a cabin.

Hyram insisted on taking a look. The two men rode in Billy's old Chevy pickup down to the bottom of Henderson Hill and turned onto an unmarked dirt road that penetrated deep into what used to be Harrison Quimby's land.

"I've never been out here before." They were the first words Hyram had uttered since leaving the driveway. It wasn't a question so Billy just kept quiet for the next few minutes. When the truck began rolling over deep horizontal ruts cutting across the road, Billy downshifted and slowed. They were getting close.

"I grew up out here. My folks had the cabin. This is where we grew tomatoes," Billy said as he pulled up to a broad, flat clearing.

The ground was hard, Hyram noted, but there was no sawgrass in sight. That was a good sign. It meant the land wasn't prone to flooding. The cabin was larger than he had expected. The outer walls were clapboard, browned by the sun and rain but in otherwise excellent condition. The roof was metal. Its edges were bent and worn in places, but Billy had recently painted it green so it looked substantial. Hyram made a note to look for signs of leakage inside.

A covered porch shaded the front door. Porches usually rotted off within a year or two, so most people who built cabins didn't bother with them. When the two men stepped up onto Billy's porch, the wood beneath their feet neither moved nor creaked. Solid, steady, and without any nails sticking out, the entrance to Billy's home was not so much a surprise to Hyram as it was an affirmation.

Billy was a meticulous housekeeper, for a man. He wasn't embarrassed to show his future father-in-law every detail of the place. "It needs a little cleanup before I let Abbie see it. Some curtains. A rug. The walls creak a little when the weather is bad but the roof and the windows are tight. And it's warm in the winter."

"How long have you lived here?" The question carried more questions behind it.

"I think we moved in right after the stock market crashed, around nineteen thirty. So I guess I've lived here for about eleven years."

"It's not an uncomfortable place," Hyram tried to be complementary. "In fact, it's a bit larger than I had imagined. How much do you pay in rent?"

"I don't pay any rent. This place was all my daddy had when he died, so he left it to me."

Hyram didn't understand how a man who ran a tomato stand could afford to buy any land at all, much less a not-too-small cabin on the corner of a two acre clearing. But his mind wasn't on finances that afternoon. He was evaluating his daughter's future husband and her future home. There was little point in prolonging the inspection.

One question bothered Hyram and he was almost sorry he had to ask it. "Has Abigail been out here, Billy?"

"No sir. No. That wouldn't be right."

Hyram was pleased Billy knew better. An unsupervised visit by an underage girl to an unmarried man's house would have been the seed of a scandal.

"Well," he sighed, pausing to look around one final time. "It'll do."

ॐ

Mrs. Northbridge insisted on delaying the wedding until after her daughter turned eighteen. There would be a birthday party on December tenth, and a bridal shower on Saturday (the thirteenth), and the wedding on Sunday, and then the honeymoon – a week in Natchez.

Hyram pointed out that a week in Natchez was far too extravagant, especially in such uncertain times. In retaliation for bringing up the financial side of his daughter's wedding, he was assigned the task of organizing a chivaree.

Subsequently, he kept his mouth shut about the selection of Sunday as the wedding day. Grace Missionary Baptist Church held all day services on Sunday.

Eventually, what was obvious to everybody else was mentioned to Mrs. Northbridge. She moved the nuptials to Saturday and canceled the bridal shower. It had become too much of a social burden, anyway, asking the same people to bring gifts to the same girl twice in one week.

Hyram spent much of his free time in the company of the groom. He liked Billy Dare. They had come to trust one another and to speak freely. Neither man drank anything stronger than coffee, but they consumed gallons of the stuff whenever they got together (usually over breakfast at the Passable Grill).

They talked about politics and Hitler and waiting for war. The Brits were fighting Germany and waiting for the United States to join the fray and end this thing like they did in 1917. Canada was fighting and waiting. France had fallen and was still waiting.

On Sunday, three days before Abbie's birthday, Japan got tired of waiting. December seventh came and went and the calendar stopped. Suddenly nobody wanted to wait any longer. Roosevelt declared war and Congress fell in behind him.

Mrs. Northbridge acted as though nothing had happened. There was a birthday party to tend to and a wedding dress that needed final fitting. Tuesday morning, she took Abigail into Passable.

First, they stopped by the Penney's store to buy paper bunting and powdered cocoa. To their surprise, the store was crowded with shoppers. Many of them were expected to be at the birthday party tomorrow.

Mrs. Northbridge found the cocoa powder easily but it was out of reach. Everything in that section of the store was out of reach, eclipsed by the expansive blue dress covering the torso of Miss Amanda Freedown.

Abbie watched, bemused, as her mother tried reaching around the infamous Freedown hips. Mrs. Northbridge really didn't want to engage the woman in conversation, but she feared that if she didn't speak up, Amanda might block access to the cocoa forever, or worse yet, back up and trap her between cans of lard and onrushing waves of blue-draped flesh.

"Pardon me, Amanda," she squeaked.

"OH! Mrs. Nooorrthbridge!" Amanda exclaimed in her best nasal singing voice. "And our little Abigail! Oh, dear me, isn't it just horrible…"

She went on about the damnable Japanese and the damnable Germans and that damnable Roosevelt. "We're at war now, you know," she explained. "There's a meeting at the Passable Mason's tomorrow to help organize a relief drive for Great Britain. God knows the president won't lift a finger to help. And all those fine young boys in Pearl Harbor, killed like that!"

Amanda's overbearing opinion struck a sour chord with Mrs. Northbridge. She had voted for Roosevelt every time. She made a mental note to serve Amanda extra-small portions at the birthday party.

Amanda snuffled into her kerchief and then begged to be excused from the birthday party, offering as a reason that she "couldn't, just *couldn't*", and then trotted away in too-tight shoes.

So went the rest of the morning. One by one, Mrs. Northbridge listened as the polite ladies of Passable extended their regrets and withdrew from her daughter's eighteenth birthday.

Her luck changed for the worse that afternoon. She and Abigail made the two-hour drive to Meridian with the radio turned off. They planned to pick up the wedding dress at *Queen City Gown* and go straight home and they didn't want to have to listen to the news all day.

Jean Phillips, the owner of Queen City Gown, was waiting on a customer when the Northbridge women arrived. She looked shocked to see them. Her expression was a bad sign.

"Missus Northbridge, how are you today? Abigail?" Her eyes told them all they needed to know. The gown wasn't going to be ready in time. "I'm so terribly, terribly sorry, ladies, but Abbie's gown isn't finished and there's nothing I can do without a seamstress and the only I had has gone missing all week, ever since Saturday morning, and you know she was Japanese so now the rumors are starting and I can't finish everything by myself, you know…"

Eventually, Jean ran of breath and excuses and decided not to charge Mrs. Northbridge for the work done so far. Mrs. Northbridge left the shop with the unfinished bridal gown slung across Abbie's arms. She'd just have to finish it herself. Abbie didn't complain. This was Tuesday and the next day she would officially be an adult. She held the dress on her lap and brushed her hand across its startling white pleats, letting her fingertips dream of a perfect wedding.

"I want ice cream," she announced. They parked in front of the Kress, went in and ordered ice cream sodas. Ice cream sodas from Kress were a rare treat, an unexpected expense readily borne and never regretted. They paid with coins both women gleaned from the depths of their purses. Not a single tear flowed during the drive home.

෯ஂஓ

Mrs. Northbridge refused to cancel the party just because the guests had all sent their regrets. Besides, she had paid for bunting and cocoa, and there was nothing else planned for today. The tables and windows were decorated in a festive rainbow of birthday colors, and a chocolate cake was set in the oven to bake.

By six-thirty in the morning, Mrs. Northbridge had single-handedly completed preparations for Abbie's birthday party. Her daughter needed sleep, so she didn't disturb her until nine o'clock.

Mrs. Northbridge needed a couple of hours alone with her exhausted thoughts while the cake cooled. When Abbie woke up, she volunteered to spread the icing, and her mother decided it would be all right to help out with her own birthday cake, just this once.

Shortly before lunchtime, the familiar sound of Billy's truck could be heard coming down the road. The party wasn't supposed to start until two, and neither of the Northbridge women had thought to call Billy and tell him there might have been a change in plans.

Billy wasn't smiling when he got out of the truck. His right hand gripped an envelope. Something in his face hinted at trouble.

"Billy, you're early," Mrs. Northbridge called out.

"I need to talk to Hyram," Billy answered glumly. "Is he in?"

"He's out back in the garden, sweetie. Are you staying for lunch?"

Billy shook his head and walked around the porch to the back of the house. Hyram was clearing weeds from their small vegetable garden. "Hi, boy," he said.

"Hyram."

"You're early, but I doubt that anybody's coming to the party, anyway."

Billy didn't seem to hear him. He shook the envelope and said, "We got a problem."

Hyram took the telegram and read it over, twice. "Is this right?" he asked. "I thought you were a '2A'. Says here your status is '1A'."

"I didn't think nothin' of it when I registered, Hyram. Hell, that was last year! "

"Well, this can't stand. We'll write to the draft board and get you reclassified."

Billy shook his head. "Won't do no good," he pointed out. "I showed this to the postmaster and he said that I'd have to report for induction before my letter ever gets to the board."

Hyram handed the draft notice back. "Have you told Abbie?"

"No. Not yet."

"She's in the house. You better get to it."

Billy didn't thank Hyram for his time. He just turned and let his feet take him into the house, unannounced. He stood in the living room, twisting the corner of his draft notice. The women were busy in the kitchen, decorating the cake. 'HAPPY B' was already spelled out, but when they saw his expression they stopped.

Mrs. Northbridge nudged Abbie and quietly told her, "Go talk to him. I see trouble."

Abigail wiped her hands and hurried into the living room. She managed a quick peck on Billy's cheek before he guided her into a chair. He said something that Mrs. Northbridge couldn't hear, and handed her the envelope. Abbie pulled out the letter, dropped it on the floor and ran to her room.

Hyram came into the kitchen and cornered his wife. "Billy has to go into the Army. He got his draft notice today. He leaves Saturday."

"No! That's the wedding!" The color drained from her face at each word. Then she saw the selfishness of her response and suddenly the wedding wasn't as important as Abbie's happiness. "They can't possibly take Billy so soon. Hyram, how can the Army...?"

"We're at war," he stated.

"Hyram. They can't do this. They can't."

It dawned on Hyram that there was a way out of this mess, but only if he could get the local government to move as quickly than the Army had. Hyram hugged his wife and told her, "Missus Northbridge, go get your coat and meet me in the car. We have work to do."

Mrs. Northbridge took one quick look in the hallway mirror on their way out, brushing off a stray smudge of flour dust from her temple. As she slid into the passenger side of the car, Hyram came out of the house with Billy and Abigail.

Abbie joined her mother in the car. Hyram pointed at the truck and told Billy, "Follow us."

"What's going on, Hyram?" Billy asked.

Hyram had the look of a man steeling himself for a fight he knew he would probably lose. "We're gonna take care of this business, boy."

Billy knew better than to pry too deeply when Hyram was in the middle of a plan. He started the old Chevy truck and fell in behind their brown Dodge. Every now and then, Abbie would turn around and look his way.

They entered Passable during the lunch hour traffic. Hyram pulled into the first open parking spot he could find at the county courthouse. Billy stopped next to the East entrance. Hyram soon joined him, without the women.

Side by side, Hyram Northbridge and William Dare marched through the courthouse door, past the sign that announced "Selective Service Board". A hand-written sign was taped beneath it, "Appeals, Room 102a".

Room 102A was the next door on the left. A line of five young men formed up outside the appeals office. Billy recognized two of them, people of low character, given to excessive drinking and general troublemaking. Zeb Cousins was at the head of the line, showing six days' stubble and wearing clothes that had recently been used to clean an engine. The next-to-last man in line, Andrew Darling, was a known petty thief and laggard.

"Are you ready?" Hyram asked, putting a large, reassuring hand on Billy's shoulder.

"Yes sir."

"Let's get this problem behind us."

Billy stepped into the waiting appeals line and Hyram stood next to him. The line moved slowly. Zeb Mason disappeared into the office and presented his case. Fifteen minutes passed before he came back out, victoriously waving his brand new "4-F" deferment in Andy Darling's face.

"Hyram," Billy said, "it don't look like I'm gonna get a hearing before lunchtime. I can stay here while you join the ladies. I'll catch up when I'm done."

Hyram tapped him on the arm and pointed to a door across the hallway. "That's Judge Greenmeyer's office," he told Billy. "Let's go talk to him and see what he can do to pull some strings."

Reluctantly, Billy gave up his place in the appeals line. Hyram had a point. Judge Greenmeyer knew a lot of important people. Maybe he had some influence with the appeals board. Billy pulled the judge's heavy oak door open, and was surprised to find Mrs. Northbridge and Abigail waiting on the other side. In front of them stood the thin gray figure of Harold Greenmeyer, Justice of the Peace.

"'Bout time you got here, Hyram," the judge joked. "As I understand it, these two children have to get married."

"Don't start any gossip, Harold," Hyram replied. "Abigail is of age and in a hurry. Let's get on with the elopement."

Five minutes later, Mrs. Northbridge's plans for her daughter's wedding were permanently deferred. She was a weepy mess all the way home, unable to speak more than two words to Hyram without an attack of the snuffles.

Abbie rode home in the truck, repeating to herself, "*Wife. I'm his wife.,*" the words described her now, but she felt no different. It was a foreign word, one she had never used to describe her own self, and yet she could hardly wait to use the word. She looked at Billy and saw no emotion at all. He just sat there, silently driving them home. No, not home. She no longer lived at home.

"*Husband,*" Billy silently tested the word. "*How did that happen?*" He had to concentrate in order to keep the truck on the road but the H-word wouldn't leave him alone.

He wished Abbie would say something. Anything. The drive back was terrifyingly quiet. He wasn't sure he was ready to be a husband. "*Too late,*" he thought, parking outside the Northbridge house.

Hyram and Billy had a long private talk in the living room. Abigail and her mother had a long private talk in the bedroom as they packed a suitcase. Shortly after one o'clock, everybody had a slice of "Happy B" cake.

Mr. and Mrs. Northbridge waved from the porch as Mr. and Mrs. Dare drove off on their two-day honeymoon at the Meridian Hotel, courtesy of Judge Greenmeyer and a well-timed telephone call.

Two o'clock chimed in the living room. The house was quiet for the first time in years. Mr. Northbridge filled two small snifters with cooking brandy and Mrs. Northbridge started taking down the bunting.

❧ CHAPTER ELEVEN ❧

"The Army had plenty of men. They didn't need Billy, but they took him anyway."

                                        Charlotte Montgomery

Saturday morning broke with a cold gray drizzle. "You should have some luggage," she said. "Other people have luggage. There… that man over there has a suitcase."

"No, the letter said 'no personal belongings.' It said the Army would provide me with everything I'll need. It's nearly nine o'clock. I'm supposed to be here at nine o'clock."

Billy fidgeted and Abbie tightened her grip on his arm, reassuring no one. Neither of them had ever been inside the bus terminal. It was an orderly frenzy of people and the deafening sound of a hundred voices jabbering all at once. On the far side of the room, a man in a khaki uniform with stripes on his arms blew a whistle.

"Do you think that's the Staff Sergeant Luther Tomkins I'm supposed to meet?"

"I don't know," Abbie answered. "But I don't see any other soldiers in here."

"I'm gonna go ask if he's Staff Sergeant Luther Tomkins," Billy said. "You stay put. I'll be right back."

Abbie watched him walk up to the soldier from behind and tap him on the arm to get his attention. Billy was a full head taller, so when the soldier turned around to see who had dared touch him he had to tilt his head up, which made his jaw jut out in an even more menacing glower.

Billy held out the letter so the soldier could look at it, but something went wrong. The soldier jerked the envelope from Billy's hand and started cursing and yelling, sometimes exploding one-syllable words with such force that droplets of spit flew out into the air. His finger jabbed at a list on the clipboard, prodded Billy's chest, and angrily pointed at one of the buses. Billy disappeared into a Greyhound with a sign in the windshield that said "INDUCTION", the sergeant directly on his heels, screaming threats the entire way. The bus closed its doors and pulled out of the terminal and just like that, Abigail was alone.

This was far different from what she had expected. There should have been lingering kisses, lovers' promises whispered in the din. Instead, the bus just drove away. She didn't even know where. In a matter of seconds, the swirl and congestion of the bus station died. There was nothing left for her to do except drive Billy's old truck slowly back home.

Mrs. Northbridge had made herself a pimiento cheese sandwich just before the truck drove up. He lunch languished untouched as she unpacked Abbie's suitcase. Hyram got busy calling the draft board, the Army, and even Judge Greenmeyer. The judge called everyone he knew at Camp Shelby, but they hadn't received any recruits from Meridian. No one knew where Billy had been taken.

It was a long, emotional week before they heard any news. A postcard, hastily scribbled in impeccable handwriting, told them he was alive and suffering through basic training in a place called "Camp Claiborne", in the middle of Louisiana! He said he was well, but tired. He said they took away his clothes and boxed them up and sent them home. He said boot camp would last about six more weeks.

Abigail had been hoping to see him on Christmas, but the calendar wasn't going to let that happen. Neither were the Japs. The New Year brought reports of the fall of the Philippines. Thousands of British and American soldiers had been captured and marched off. There were rumors of random beheadings, and worse.

The slow weeks of worry took their toll on Abigail, days and hours and minutes constantly without Billy. She could barely remember what he looked like. Oh, how she wished she had a photograph of their wedding day. Boot camp would be finished on February the second, a distant eternity.

Hyram bought a bus ticket from Alexandria to Meridian and mailed it to Billy in the middle of January. He made certain a fresh roll of film was in the Kodak, too. That same day, Abbie convinced him to drive her down to the "Dare House", as she called it. February was getting closer and she planned to make their cabin ready so that she could be carried across the threshold right and proper.

She took two sets of fresh bed sheets and as many towels as she thought she could steal from the linen closet. Her mother put a mop and a bucket in the bed of Billy's old pickup truck, excitedly conspiring with Abbie to apply a liberal measure of "woman's touch" and turn the cabin into a home. Today, they'd just clean up and measure the windows for curtains.

The remnants of the old cabin were still smoldering when they pulled up. Abbie pressed her hands against her mouth in a vain attempt to stave off the waves of nausea. A corner post and the chimney were the only pieces still standing upright. The window glass had melted away in the intense heat, and the metal roof had collapsed in on itself.

Mrs. Northbridge put her arm around Abbie and tried to comfort her. "It's all right, sweetie," she told her. "You and Billy will live with us until you can find another place."

Hyram drove his family back home and then reported the fire to the Passable County Sheriff. The sheriff called Kennison Meeder and asked him to come out to the cabin.

The three men gathered an hour later at the burn site. Hyram asked the sheriff why his son-in-law's employer needed to be there, and learned for the first time how deeply ran the currents of Kennison Meeder's character.

"It was arson, sure enough," the sheriff pronounced after thirty seconds' investigation.

"What makes you so sure?" Kennison asked.

"I can smell it. Kerosene," the sheriff answered. He walked around the outside of the cabin, wiping his fingers against the burnt walls and sniffing them. When he got to the front of the cabin he pointed at the ashes that were once the porch and called out, "Here. This is where it started. Yessir, this here fire was started on purpose." A Passable County fire truck came out and the fire chief confirmed the sheriff's opinion.

The cabin had burned quickly, leaving little behind to salvage. The contents that could be identified were removed piece-by-piece, written on a list and set on the ground. Within an hour, Billy's life story was laid out in a short row beside the charred embers of his home – bedsprings and a sink and an ironing board and a blackened iron. Not much else survived.

None of Orvis' tools were found in the fire. Nobody but Billy knew they had been there, hidden away in an ancient, rotting canvas tool bag under his bed. The thief couldn't know their true value. He would open the satchel and see old, worn out tools. Only Billy had the power to look inside and see Orvis Dare looking back. The tools were his secret treasure, and they were the greatest loss of all.

✢ CHAPTER TWELVE ❧

"For Abbie, the hardest part was getting used to being without Billy. For Hyram, the worst of it was the helplessness."
Charlotte Montgomery

The Solomon Islands were invaded a week before Billy finished boot camp. Four days later, Abbie received another letter from Camp Claiborne. All that was in the envelope was the bus ticket. Written on the back in neat block print was the message;

"SORRY. CAN'T COME HOME. LOVE BILLY"

Hyram, of course, was furious. He drove straight to the courthouse and angrily shoved the door open into Judge Greenmeyer's courtroom.

"Damn it, Harold…"

Reflexes took over and Hyram shut his mouth. Rows of people quietly observing the narratives of the McCordle divorce turned in chorus line unison and stared at the intruder. The plaintiff's lawyer failed to notice the change and continued dryly describing a belt whipping administered to his client by her husband. Judge Greenmeyer held up one hand, quieting the lawyer and halting the bailiff, who was advancing on Hyram with a nightstick at the ready.

"Good morning, Hyram," Judge Greenmeyer said during the lull. "Something on your mind?"

"It… it can wait," was Hyram's sheepish reply.

"No, by all means, draw nigh and present your request to the court," the judge insisted.

"It's about my boy, Billy," Hyram started.

The judge stared at Hyram, gestured for him to come closer and said, "Sidebar." Hyram didn't know the word and assumed the judge must have been talking to someone else, so he didn't move.

"Mister Northbridge, 'sidebar' means come on up here so that we can talk in private." Hyram did as he was told, walking up to the judge and leaning on his judicial bench. "What's on your mind, Hyram?"

"We got no idea where the Army took him and now they won't tell us," he told the judge, irritation in his voice.

"And what do you want me to do about it?"

"I don't know," Hyram confessed, adding, "I just thought you might know someone."

"Well, I heard Senator Wall Doxey is in town for a few days. You might drive down there and look for him. He'd be at the new Meridian post office, top floor."

"Thanks, Harold." Hyram headed toward the exit.

"Good luck, Hyram. Bailiff, detain Mr. Northbridge," the judge ordered. The bailiff still held his club, but Hyram exercised good manners and stopped voluntarily. "Harold Northbridge, I find you in contempt of court and order the bailiff to collect a fine of five dollars." BAM! His gavel made the order final. "Please be more circumspect the next time you enter my courtroom. I won't tolerate rudeness or foul language. Tell Wall I said 'Hello'."

❧

Hyram paid his fine and drove two hours to Meridian. He parked at the 9th Street post office and rode the elevator to the top floor. With Billy's postcards and the bus ticket clenched in his fist, he charged into the public congressional office to demand action.

He stopped at the reception desk and briefly explained his situation to the slender man seated there. The clerk's white hair made him look older than he was. "My boy, my son-in-law," Hyram stammered, "was took by the Army and now can't come home!"

The clerk took the bus ticket and looked at it carefully. "What would you like me to do about it?" he asked.

"I don't want *you* to do anything!" he brayed. "I want to talk to Senator Doxey and get *him* to find out where my daughter's husband is!"

The clerk stood and walked over to Hyram's side of the desk and stuck out his hand. "At your service."

"What?" Hyram asked.

The clerk repeated his greeting, "Wall Doxey. At your service."

"*Senator* Wall Doxey? United States Senator..."

"Doxey, yes. That's me."

Hyram looked at the man suspiciously, not sure whether to take him at his word or run and find a policeman. "You're the senator?"

"I was this morning."

Hyram's eyes widened. "How do I know for sure that you're the senator?"

"If you need proof, you can go downstairs and ask anyone to come up here and identify me. I'll wait." The offer alone was good enough for Hyram and he finally shook Senator Doxey's hand. "All of my interns have run off and joined up, so I'm alone up here," he explained.

Senator Doxey listened patiently as Hyram told how Billy had been drafted, ruining Christmas, and how he couldn't even get any mail out.

"And now, this!" Hyram poked at the bus ticket before sliding it into his coat pocket.

"Save that if you can," the senator said. "A soldier might be given a 3-day pass with little or no advance notice. Perhaps your daughter could use the ticket to travel out to Camp Claiborne."

"But he's not at Claiborne any more," Hyram said. "We don't know where he's gone or what he's doing."

"I'm sorry, Mister Northbridge, but that's War Department business." Senator Doxey went on to explain that troops were forbidden to divulge their whereabouts, their destinations, or their travel plans. Censors would read every piece of mail and cut out sensitive information. "Letters from your boy," he said, "will be strictly regulated."

"You don't understand. We don't seem to be getting any mail at all."

"But you did get mail," the senator argued. "Are those cards from William?" He lifted them from Hyram's hand and read them one after the other. With a puzzled look, he examined at them more closely.

"Mister Northbridge...Hyram, forgive me if I'm intruding on a private subject..."

"What?" Hyram asked. "What subject?"

"It's just that these postcards... Sir, have you looked at these?"

"Of course." Then he paused and said, "Well, no. Abbie, my girl, she read them to us. They were addressed to her, after all."

The senator handed the letters back to him. "Hyram, take a moment and look at these closely."

He did as the senator asked, but he had already listened to Billy's words read out to him over and over. "I don't understand, Mister Doxey. What am I supposed to be reading?"

"Don't *read* them, Hyram. *Look* at them."

"I still don't..." Hyram shook his head.

"The handwriting is different," Senator Doxey pointed out, touching each postcard with his finger. "The penmanship changes from card to card. These were written by different people, sir."

Hyram turned the cards over and over. The only sound in the room was the flipping of the stiff paper. He looked front and back, and then to the front again. His face showed nothing but confusion.

"You won't be getting a lot of letters, Hyram," the senator said. "Your son-in-law can't write."

"But, that can't be. These postcards... I mean, he's smart. He said his mother taught him to read and write when he was a boy."

"I didn't mean to imply that he isn't smart. That has nothing to do with it, sir. He could've been taught, then maybe he never got around to using what he learned. There's lots of reasons why he might need help writing home. "

Hyram shook the handful of postcards. "I just can't believe he's illiterate. I've seen him write figures when he's estimating work."

"That's not unusual, Hyram. But figures aren't letters and words and such." The senator got up and walked back over behind his desk. "Sometimes, it's like this. Folks who don't read or write get embarrassed about their shortcoming, so to avoid feeling bad they just quit writing."

Hyram agreed with the senator's opinion. "I don't know about it bein' a shortcoming. I think he doesn't write because the Army doesn't let him."

"I can understand your disdain, Mr. Northbridge. It's obvious that your Billy is a very likeable individual. After all, he talked at least three other people into writing these notes," he chuckled. "But the Army has a program for teaching a soldier basic reading and writing skills. I know that he's a mite busy with the war and all, but if your son-in-law is as bright as you say, you'll see the change in his letters."

"I'd just like to see *more* letters," Hyram slipped the cards back into his coat pocket and stood to leave, his shoulders slumped. "Well, senator, I guess there's nothing either of us can do. I wish I could tell my daughter where her husband has gone. Thank you for your time."

Days like this made Wall feel old and tired. He loved being a senator. He was a public figure and people sought him out and asked for his help. And he was important enough that he could pick up the telephone and make things happen.

"Hyram, I'm due in Washington in two days' time, and I'm going to be too busy to help you once I'm there. But I'm in Mississippi today, and I think I might know someone who could help us find your son-in-law. Give me just a minute." He motioned for Hyram to sit back down, but remained standing himself.

The senator picked up the phone. "Hello operator? Long distance, please." Wall tapped his toes on the bare floor as he waited. "Hello operator? Connect me to the switchboard at the Pentagon, please? Yes, *that* Pentagon – station to station is all right, thank you."

The senator tilted his head back slightly as he talked, giving his voice a nasal quality. "Good morning! Senator Wall Doxey's office calling for General Marshall. Can you put the senator through, please?" He covered the phone with his hand and winked at Hyram. "They won't put me through unless they think they're talking to my secretary."

The phone demanded his attention again. "Chief of Staff's office? I have an urgent call from Senator Wall Doxey for General Marshall. Can you connect me with his G-1, please? Yes, I'll wait."

The toe tapping resumed, then abruptly stopped. "Hello? General Haislip's office? Senator Doxey's office, holding for the assistant G-1 – Doxey – D-O-X-E-Y – yes, *THAT* Senator Doxey – thank you, I'll hold – good morning, Colonel, Wall Doxey here – I'm well, thank you for asking, but a bit short on time. Would you mind terribly transferring my call to your outer office? Thank you – hello, Sally? Wall, here – no, not until next week. Listen, Sally, I need you to violate the National Secrets Act for me, could you do that? Wonderful!

I'm trying to find the current whereabouts of Army Private William Dare – just out of boot camp a few days ago – Claiborne, Camp Claiborne – Dare, D-A-R-E – yes, I'll hold…"

"I'm impressed," Hyram said. "You haven't even asked whether I voted for you."

"Did you?"

"No. James Eastland."

"I like him," Doxey said.

A few minutes later, the phone demanded his attention again. "Yes, I'm still here." The senator pulled out a pencil and started writing on his notepad. "Uh huh – uh huh – That's fine. Thank you, Sally – next week – of course – my best to your family – Bye."

He hung up the phone and tore off the top page from the pad, handing it to Hyram. "Your boy is on a troop ship. He's headed to England."

☙ CHAPTER THIRTEEN ❧

*"The days ran together like boxcars, each one the same as the
one before. But from time to time, a circus train would go by."*
Charlotte Montgomery

Mornings were the hardest part. Soft pink skies filled her
slumbering moments with dreams of color and music and Billy
by her side. Then the sun would break over the treetops and
stream blindingly through her window, leaving Abbie no
choice but to open her eyes and drink in the grayness of
another day.

Mrs. Northbridge allowed her daughter to enjoy the
occasional foul mood, but she knew better than to permit her to
wallow in selfish sorrow. She was always looking for
something they might do together, something constructive that
could help the war effort.

The newspapers were full of stories about women going to
work at aircraft factories or becoming welders down in
Pascagoula, but those opportunities didn't extend very far
inland. They didn't build very many battleships in Passable.

One afternoon, she happened upon an article in the
Meridian Star about a ten-year old boy in Columbus who
organized a scrap metal drive. The newspaper said he
collected enough wrought iron and soft steel to build a

complete B-25 Mitchell bomber and two five hundred pound bombs. The photo showed him shaking hands with the mayor and flashing the "V" sign. In the caption, he was given honorary credit for killing more than a hundred Japs in the great Doolittle raid a month earlier.

Her eyes lit up when she showed the article to her daughter. *This* was something they could do right here at home. They discussed it briefly and decided to drive the Buick from house to house in a huge circle, alerting everybody to start boxing up their scrap war materials. A few days later, they would come back around and pick up the boxes in Billy's old truck.

Over breakfast, they discussed their plan with Hyram. He asked whether they planned to stop at every house or just a select few. Excitedly, they told him the only way to conduct a war drive was to ask *everybody* to contribute. He pointed out that their first stop would take them into Zeb Cousins' house. The wall clock in the living room ticked loudly as they considered the implications.

Two days later, Mrs. Northbridge and Mrs. Dare got into the family car and turned left, officially starting their war drive. A mile down the road, they slowed and stopped just short of the driveway to the Cousins' farm. From the safety of the Buick they could see most of the twenty acres used by Zeb and his younger half-brother Cody to occasionally grow low-grade beans and peppers. In the distance, a fatally rusted Allis-Chalmers sat for the third straight year in the middle of a small field of corn stalks. The house squatted on the edge of an overgrown clearing, next to a double-jointed wooden barn sagging under the weight of its own boards.

"We can go to the next house," Mrs. Northbridge suggested.

"And how would that look?" Abigail protested weakly. "People will talk. They'll say we skipped over the Cousins' place because we thought he was white trash."

"He *is* white trash, dear."

"Well, to his credit, he hasn't murdered anyone."

"We might be his first," her mother argued.

"Well, if he tries to kill *me*, you'll to come to my defense. And if he tries to kill *you*, I'll run get help," Abbie said.

They were as prepared as they could be, under the circumstances. Zebulon Cousins answered his door after their first delicate knock.

"Ladies!" he beamed. Zeb was given to chewing tobacco with the few teeth remaining in his jaw, and when he opened his door to admit the visitors, a thin line of brown drool took flight and escaped through his facial stubble, slowly weaving its way to freedom. A man of refinement, Zeb caught the errant saliva with his bare forearm before it could become an embarrassment.

"Well! Mrs. Northbridge and Abbie! What brings y'all out this way?" He brushed a cat off his sofa and gestured to the ladies to make themselves at home.

Mrs. Northbridge took the initiative. "We're collecting for the war effort, Zeb."

"That's fine. Yessir, ain't that just *fine*." He fluffed a cushion, releasing a soft cloud of gray that hovered over the couch. "Won't you ladies siddown for awhile," he offered. Abigail covered her mouth and nose with ill-disguised revulsion. Neither lady sat. After a few seconds, the cat returned to its indentation on the couch and Zeb's invitation was allowed to expire on its own.

"Well, how kin I help?" he asked.

Mrs. Northbridge turned to her daughter and passed control of the conversation. "Mrs. Dare?"

"What?" Abbie asked.

"Answer the gentleman, dear," Mrs. Northbridge smiled, nodding in Zeb's direction. "What are we collecting?"

Neither Abigail nor her mother had any notion of what the United States government might need from them at that instant. "Oh, mister Cousins," she laughed. "I'm sure that whatever you have to offer will be graciously received by the War Department." Her girlish optimism, unfortunately, inspired him.

"Well, ladies..." he paused for a second of serious thought, "...I s'pose I kin come up with somethin'." This made Mrs. Northbridge grin with pride.

"But yer drivin' Hyram's car, ain't ya?" Zeb observed. "I'm 'fraid that some of my con-ter-bew-shuns may be a tad dusty. Why don't I just put a few things into my pickup and drop 'em off at your place later in the week? How would that suit ya?"

Anything that offered the opportunity to avoid a return visit suited them just fine. They thanked Zeb and took their leave, accepting him at his word he would tell all his friends about the scrap drive.

Thus began the rape of Hyram Northbridge's garden.

On Friday morning, Hyram awoke to discover Zeb Cousins had come by in the dark of night and deposited his contributions in the middle of the pea patch. He was both shocked and impressed by the sheer volume of work Zeb had accomplished gathering, transporting, and offloading so much material in such a short span of time by moonlight without making any noise.

A quick scan of Zeb's donations told him that the toothless man had used his own judgment in the selection of war materials, taking generous liberties with the definition of "scrap". In short, Zebulon Cousins had cleaned out his barn and brought the contents into Hyram's vegetable garden.

In the center of the pile was a mule-drawn mower, rusted solid; a cast iron sink; a bag of old underwear; rotting leather harnesses; a chair without one of its legs; another chair with four legs but no back; rusting hammers, nails, screwdrivers, awls, shovels, and axes; two dozen fence posts, all rotten; a bale of barbed wire, hopelessly tangled; a wooden bucket with several bullet holes in it; something that looked like old socks; several pieces of rough-hewn lumber, warped and bristling with nails.

Hyram gave up trying to identify Zeb's contributions after finding the dried up remains of what might once have been a rat, or perhaps a shoe. He bundled Mrs. Northbridge and

Abigail into the car and headed to the Cousins' place, hoping to return the donations and ask Zeb to come retrieve all his war materials.

Nobody answered the door. Zeb's ancient Farmall tractor was missing. So was his trailer. Hyram quickly forged a mental image too obscene for words. He mashed the accelerator pedal as hard as he dared, hurrying back to his home, racing time and the overflowing generosity of Zeb Cousins.

As he pulled into his driveway, he saw it was too late. "Hyram's Garden" had become the rally cry for every farm within ten miles. His objections were misunderstood, garnering a round of earnest applause and heralding the arrival of three more tractors and two pickup trucks, all driven by patriotic farmers anxious to unburden their barns and cellars and help Abbie's husband fight the Germans.

Zeb was in the process of unloading his second trailer full of critical war materials. He would have finished earlier except he had to wait for Cody to unhitch a two-seat buckboard wagon he was donating. Neither man wasted energy analyzing what the military might want with a ten-year-old rotted wood wagon. One of its wheels collapsed in the soft soil of Hyram's garden.

The brothers decided to leave it there, filled to capacity with broken window glass, assorted rusting soup cans and an ancient, empty, rotting canvas tool bag.

❧ CHAPTER FOURTEEN ❧

"Letters from Billy always meant one thing. He was alive."
Charlotte Montgomery

The mails were slow, but they could always be slower. Every letter Billy sent home went through a censor first. Any mention of where he was or where he thought he might be going was either blacked out or cut out with a razor blade.

Billy was in England. Abigail knew that much for certain. He was in England and he was safe. He still didn't write home as much as Abbie wanted, and his letters were painfully short. But he was safe in England.

The newspapers wrote about battles in places like Midway and Tobruk, Guadalcanal and El Alamein. Letters from Billy just said he was all right and "don't worry".

She didn't worry. Not too much. England was the safest place to be if you had to be over there. The war news was mostly about fighting in the Pacific and North Africa, and it looked like Russia would fall to Germany very soon.

Abigail wrote to Billy every day, even though reading was probably a struggle for him. She told him about how Hyram's garden was larger this year, a full-fledged Victory Garden. She told him the story of the scrap metal drive. Every bit of gossip that might be remotely interesting found its way into her letters. She didn't say anything about the burning of the cabin.

Billy wrote back, saying he was all right and not to worry.

Abbie wrote about having to change her first flat tire while driving to Passable in the old pickup truck. She told Billy about an argument she had with the checkout girl at Breen's Rexall. She told him about a fuss brewed up by the Klan in Irondale, something about training Negroes to fly fighters in combat, and how Kennison Meeder took exception to an epithet Cody Cousins said and threw a rock at him, with good effect.

She left out any mention of the new gold stars that hung in the windows of Passable.

Billy wrote back. He was all right. Don't worry.

Thanksgiving without Billy was lonely, she told him. Hyram took her deer hunting for the first time but she didn't even see a deer, she wrote. The nights fell earlier and she went to bed earlier and when she woke up in the morning her first thoughts were of him, her letters said.

Billy wrote back, wishing everyone a merry Christmas and telling Abbie not to worry.

By the end 1942, the newspapers and the radio were full of opinions about was how unbeatable the Germans were. A month later, Rommel's Afrikakorps lay defeated and Field Marshal Paulus' 6th Army surrendered to the Russians at Stalingrad. In May, the U-boat threat had been removed from the Atlantic, making England safer than ever for Billy.

The summer of 1943 brought news of the invasion of Sicily and the capture of Messina. Mussolini was hanged and then shot. Italy fell.

Abbie wrote to Billy every day. Not much was happening in Passable. Ron Daly sold his garage to a company in Jackson and the new owners hired him right back to run the new gas station and sell Esso. The FBI came by the house and took her wedding dress as evidence against a Japanese national, Myuki Tanamura. She didn't know whether she'd ever get the dress back.

There were no letters from Billy in July. This worried Abbie, even though her mother told her that it probably didn't mean anything. August passed with no letters from England. She ignored her mother and worried anyway.

The only thing she found that could ease her mood was the simple act of sweeping the kitchen. She organized the floor into broad swaths and pulled the broom along each one, gathering small levies of dust and foot-dirt, racing each other side by side to the far wall.

Sweeping gave her time to think about absolutely nothing. Worrying about Billy burned at her every day, so she picked up the broom and swept. And when that no longer worked, Abbie wiped down the refrigerator and cleaned the sink and washed the dishes. And in the fading light of summer dusk, she wrote letters to Billy every day.

He hadn't written back for nearly ten weeks. Abbie woke up worried and went to bed worried and woke up the next morning ready to clean the windows and wipe down high places for dust. The Northbridge home had never been so spotless. It was always ready to entertain visitors.

In early September, Abigail was alone in the house when a black sedan turned into their driveway. She didn't see it pull up, and her mother was out back tending to the garden with Hyram. The first indication that Abbie was no longer alone in the house was a sharp knock on the front door – a man's knock, insistent but tentative, testing whether anyone was home.

The house was immaculate. She had even taken the time this morning to wipe down the screen door. Proud of her spotless home, she opened the front door.

An Army officer stood there, stiff and formal, carrying an envelope and a Bible. In a flicker, the purpose of his visit was clear. A lifetime of loneliness stabbed at her heart as she stared at his uniform. The tiny gold cross on his lapel became a pinpoint of light drowning all else in darkness.

Her head throbbed. Looking up at the ceiling, she could hear the thump of her own pulse. Her fainting episode had not been cleanly executed. Instead of waking up on the couch, legs crossed in a ladylike pose, she was sprawled on the freshly swept kitchen floor. Mrs. Northbridge held a damp cloth against Abigail's brow, trying to cool the swelling knot she earned colliding with the sparkling clean refrigerator on her way down.

"Billy…" her voice was weak.

"Sshhh," Mrs. Northbridge tried to keep her still. "Billy is all right. He's alive."

"But the Chaplain…"

"Lost," Mrs. Northbridge explained. "He was lost, sweetie. He stopped for directions. That's all. He's never been to Passable before."

"Lost…?" Abigail laughed weakly. "Lost."

Two weeks later, they received a letter from Billy. It was thicker than usual, and stiff like cardboard. Abigail ripped at the envelope and pulled out a single, small photograph. She stared at it for several seconds and then held it against her forehead before passing it to Mrs. Northbridge and Hyram.

It was a simple black-and-white photograph of three soldiers on a city street. Rifles were slung across their shoulders. Helmets sat on their heads, cocked slightly to one side. The men looked happy. Scrawled across the bottom in childlike block print was "ROME 1943", and beneath that, "Love Bill".

Hyram's eyes were suddenly filled with tears and he passed the photo back to Abbie. "What's wrong, Dad?" she asked. She couldn't remember the last time she had seen her father cry.

He wiped his eyes and blew his nose. "Nothing," he said, "nothing. It's just that, well, the writing is different, that's all."

The two women huddled and examined the photo more carefully. Mrs. Northbridge said, "It sure is. It looks awful, like he wrote it with his feet!"

Hyram had never felt so close to his son-in-law. He didn't know why he was so sure, but this photo was all the proof he needed. "Don't you see? Billy wrote it himself. He didn't get any help this time."

Letters started coming more frequently, but just barely so and the content of his notes was painfully sparse. Billy was back in England, safe again, and although he now had time to write down his own words, writing was a struggle for him. As a result he usually ended up saying very little. Abigail kept every letter, reading them over and over late at night when the house was still.

On the first of June 1944, the mails contained another letter from Billy. It was short and troubling. She turned it over and looked at the back, hoping for more but finding only blank paper. "I don't understand," she told her family.

"Read it," Mrs. Northbridge insisted.

Abigail read the letter out loud;

"CANT RITE FOR WHILE – PRAY – LOVE, BILL"

"Oh," Hyram said. "He's getting ready for something big."

"I don't know what it could be," Mrs. Northbridge argued. "This letter is over two weeks old. We'd have heard something on the radio by now."

Five days later, Billy Dare pushed past two other soldiers and took cover behind a crumbling concrete wall on a beach in France. He was following a sergeant he had never met and trying hard to be as small as possible. He had a clean rifle in his hands and eighty rounds of ammunition. He was scared, but he wasn't worried.

Two weeks after the invasion of Normandy, Abigail Dare opened a cream-colored envelope with nothing inside. Then she noticed the envelope itself opened up and had a note scribbled in the center. Written in pencil, it said;

"MADE IT. LOVE BILL"

It was three months before she received another letter, but that one was too heavily censored to make any sense out of it at all. A much longer letter followed, just in time for Abbie's twenty-first birthday. It was filled with hopeful news. The Germans weren't so tough, after all. Billy had been transferred to the 14th Cavalry, which struck Mrs. Northbridge as funny.

"Are we still fighting Indians?" she asked.

Less than a week before Christmas, the kitchen radio bristled with news about a German breakout in the Ardennes. The names of the towns sounded lonely and distant. In the Schnee Eifel Mountains, German Panzers charged the American lines with desperate boldness. The 14th Cavalry was spread thin, but they fought hard to give other units time to escape. After three days of combat, the 14th no longer existed.

There would be no more letters from Billy.

The battle went badly for the Germans, but neither side could say with any certainty how many men had been lost. A month after the fall of the 14th Cavalry, the Army released the official casualty count, five thousand men. By March, they had amended that number to ten thousand. Then they doubled the March estimate. Then they doubled it again. And then again.

Ninety thousand Americans had been killed or wounded during the month-long fighting in the Ardennes. No one knew how many had surrendered, although the Red Cross did its best to organize prisoner information into lists.

The bureaucratic machine that powered all wars was breaking down in Germany. Without accountability, the defenders became beasts, abusing and even executing their prisoners. The atrocities took on the names of towns like Malmedy, Aushwitz, and Buchenwald.

Hyram listened attentively to the radio reports of the German extermination camps. The imagery was horrific – bodies littering the ground, cremation ovens stuffed with human skeletons, gas chambers. He choked on his own disgust as detached voices described the cold, graphic horror of the war in Europe.

The sickness of the daily radio war was ripping at his family, as well. The look in Abigail's eyes told him she couldn't take much more. The little brown box crackled with fresh, terrifying news. "We interrupt this program…"

He clicked the radio off and reached deep into his pants pocket, pulling out a small handful of change and a five-dollar bill. "Let's drive to town for supper," he suggested.

Mrs. Northbridge objected. "Hyram, that's so extravagant! No. Besides, it's late… nearly two o'clock."

He took Abbie by the hand and started toward the door, saying, "Mrs. Northbridge. I am taking our daughter to town for a store-bought meal. You are invited to accompany us if you wish." He put on his hat and finished, "Or you can stay here and wash dishes."

She ran to catch up, grinning.

It was good to get away. The town bustled with activity. Hyram had to park around the corner from the Passable Grill, but the weather was soft and pleasant, and the short walk lifted their spirits.

The grill was unusually crowded. They found a table near the door and waited to be served. "Something's wrong," Abigail whispered. "Nobody is talking."

"And there's too many people in here," Hyram added. "What's today? Thursday? Look over there," he pointed to a group of men sitting at the lunch counter. "That's Hilton Sanford. What is he doing here? He hasn't taken time off from work since his wife passed away. And over there, that's George Hoy, the principal – on a school day!"

The waitress slipped between the chairs and placed three menus on the table without saying a word. Her eyes were bloodshot. Hyram stopped her before she could walk away.

"Mary, what on Earth is going on? I've never seen it like this in here."

She wiped a sniffle onto her apron. "You don't know? You haven't heard?" Her voice was hoarse and strained.

"Heard what?" Abigail asked.

"The president," Mary said, quavering. "Mr. Roosevelt. He died this afternoon."

Their appetites suddenly gone, they quietly agreed to abandon their lunch plans and drive back home. Abigail broke the silence five miles later.

"Do we lose?"

"What? What's that, dear?" Mrs. Northbridge asked.

"The war. Do we lose the war?"

"No, of course not. Why would you ask such a thing?"

"Well, Mister Roosevelt is dead, but Hitler isn't. He's still alive. Doesn't he win?"

Hyram chimed in. "Not by a long shot, Abbie. We still have a president."

"Who?" she asked, "Who's the president, now?"

"It's the vice-president, of course," Hyram answered.

"What's his name?"

"It's, um… well, I can't remember right off. But I know that he's a farmer from Iowa or Idaho or somewhere like that."

"A farmer," Mrs. Northbridge said. "A farmer. Oh, God save us."

The house stayed quiet for days. The radio still interrupted its broadcast for special announcements, puncturing the peace of the Northbridge household with frightening stories: news about Bergen-Belsen and Dachau; news about the Russians and Patton and how our side was winning in Europe; news about Hitler, and how that funny little man shot himself in the head and ended the war.

The mailman brought nothing but bills and newspapers. There was no letter from Billy.

Soon enough, there was no more news about Europe. Our soldiers started coming home – one at a time, four at a time. But not Billy. The Army listed him as "missing", which only meant that nobody had found his body. Nobody was looking. Nobody cared about Europe any more. The war in the Pacific was all the radio talked about.

ೲ

The summer of 1945 brought ten gold stars into Passable County. Ten mothers would never again see their sons. There would be more.

Mrs. Northbridge visited with every family who had lost a child to this horrible war. Abigail went with her on one of these visits, but she couldn't make herself stay. All she could think about was Billy, taken from her six months ago without any ceremony, without a flag, without a funeral. There had to be thousands of Billies, littering the forests of Germany and Belgium and France. No gold stars for their families, nothing but months and years of waiting and not knowing.

Abigail felt the days brush by, barely touching her. She knew deep inside she would never again see Billy, and the damn Army wouldn't give her a gold star because they didn't even know who Billy *was*. They had never known who he was, or where he was, or even if he was alive or dead. She felt cheated, and she felt guilty for feeling cheated.

On a late summer afternoon, Mrs. Northbridge took Abbie into town to pick up a few items for the cupboard and to do a little window-shopping. During the drive, the car radio picked up the tail end of another important announcement. A new type of bomb had been used for the first time. They called it an "atom" bomb. The Army had dropped one on a city in Japan and now the entire city was gone!

Most of the town of Passable was abuzz with talk about the atom bomb. Abigail went inside the grocery with her mother and listened with indifference to the war gossip.

"Yes, the entire city..."

"...millions of Japs killed..."

"...war will be over soon..."

"...drop one right on Tokyo..."

"...damn Japs earned it..."

The voices around her droned on, but Abbie paid no attention. She let her feet take her from aisle to aisle, shopping without thinking. She was afraid to think. Afraid that if she started, the thinking would never end and she'd lose her mind.

She counted her money in front of the butcher's counter, but was twenty-four cents short for the fresh chicken she planned to cook for dinner. She let her fingertips linger on the front, lightly aware of how much colder the smooth glass felt. She looked at her reflection and saw an old woman looking back at her through wrinkled eyes. Behind the old woman, a mirror image of Passable went about its business.

In the distance, a car gunned its engine and pulled around a Greyhound bus that had stopped in the middle of the street. Passable was too small for its own station, so buses almost never stopped here. This one shifted gears and headed out of town, trailing dark gray diesel smoke.

At first, no one paid much notice of the gaunt stranger in Army khakis, a large green duffel bag at his feet. He seemed lost. Soldiers were a rare sight in Passable and this one was interesting to look at, so one by one, people looked.

Each saw something in his face, a feature they thought they recognized. They looked again. Two at a time, sometimes three, they drew closer just to be sure. Soon a small crowd formed, surrounding the soldier, touching him, speaking his name, growing and swelling and jostling and laughing.

Abigail heard the commotion and turned away from her reflection to see what was so interesting. Something inside her chest pulled her forward, closer to the crowd, dragging her closer to its center, pushing people out of the way, fighting to get to the soldier and then suddenly she was there, standing in front of him.

She barely recognized Billy Dare.

She reached for him with both arms, but when they touched, panic exploded inside her heart. She pushed Billy away and rubbed her hands against his right arm, up and down, from the elbow to the shoulder and back down to the wrist. Then she made him open his hand. Franticly, she counted his fingers and made him flex his hand into a fist. Five fingers and they all worked, and she was satisfied. Then she examined his left arm and hand, his ears, his legs, and his feet.

"You... you're OK," she stammered, letting her tears flow. She locked her arms around Billy's neck, knocking his cap from his head. "You're OK! You're OK!" she repeated, stealing time to kiss his face and his neck.

She inhaled his aroma, and he hers. On a normal day, such public affection would have landed them in front of Constable Mitzner for a stern lecture on inappropriate behavior. But the constable was already standing there in front of the crowd, grinning, so Abbie threw away modesty and let her next kisses devour Billy's mouth. God Himself could not have stopped her.

Their faces met lightly in a bashful touch, then she pressed her lips against his, kissing him hard. The crowd grew. Their cheers and applause added fire to her passion. Abbie twisted her head and jammed her mouth against Billy's, again and again.

The kiss changed in a flash of horror. Her lips pressed against his teeth and were met with a sensation of movement, a retreating emptiness. Abigail pulled back and stared at Billy, her eyes wide with shock.

He broke off contact, turned to one side and stuck a finger into his mouth. "Fa-wee," he apologized, sheepishly glancing at Abbie as he adjusted the false teeth, which had been jarred loose by the accumulated kisses.

"Your teeth..." she started.

"Gone," he said. "C'mon, let's go home."

He tried to pick up his duffel bag, but Jim Mitzner beat him to it. Abbie tugged him in the direction of the car, parked a half a block away. Someone's arm reached over Billy's shoulder and handed him his fallen garrison cap. Fifty happy hands patted his shoulders, touched his back, and pushed him along toward the car.

Mrs. Northbridge stood next to the Buick like a chauffeur, smiling broadly, standing at attention and greeting the returning soldier with a simple salute.

Billy stopped in front of her and returned the gesture, then pulled Mrs. Northbridge into a bear hug, kissed her on the cheek and whispered, "Thank you."

They crowded into the front seat, backed the car into the street and shifted gears, rolling slowly past the milling crowd. As soon as the road ahead was clear, they accelerated to a normal speed and in seconds were out of Passable.

Billy gripped Abigail's hand and wouldn't let go, but he didn't look at her and didn't speak. Instead, he just sat and gazed out the car window. She didn't press him. She knew better. There would be time for talking.

❧ CHAPTER FIFTEEN ❧

"Trapped between two worlds, one a dream and the other a nightmare, it would take time for him to become Billy again."
Charlotte Montgomery

The Germans had been thorough and efficient. His company, or what was left of it after the Panzers and Tigers were finished, marched through the thick December snow. Two days of walking, waiting, and walking some more, one soldier after another, with Billy somewhere in a line of more than five thousand captured Americans.

On either side of the endless line were German soldiers, warm in their dark gray wool. They felt no hatred toward the Americans. Neither did they feel pity. Their rifles were loaded and cocked, to save time. Trucks carrying fresh Nazi soldiers rolled up and down the line of prisoners, replacing guards before they became too tired, and reinforcing their rifles with machine guns. Any escaping prisoner would be shot, and the prisoners anywhere near him would be gunned down as well.

On the third day, Billy was marched to a farmhouse the Germans had converted into a prisoner processing facility. He waited, standing in the wet snow for four hours before being taken inside for interrogation. The German officer asking the questions spoke English badly and had no sense of humor. He passed a sheet of paper and a dull pencil across the desk, pointed at a line and ordered, "Sign the paper."

"I'm not real good at readin'," Billy told him.

"Sign, please," the officer insisted.

"You'll have to read it to me," Billy pushed the paper back at the officer and woke up on the floor, still tasting the wood and oil from the guard's rifle butt. Two more German soldiers ran into the room and lifted Billy by his armpits. He was taken back outside and dropped face down into the snow. One of the captured medics ran to his side, but the damage to his teeth had already been done.

Inside the farmhouse, the German officer crumpled Billy's unsigned prisoner identification report and tossed it into the fireplace. Corporal William Dare did not exist. Not to the Germans and not to the Red Cross.

As soon as he was able to stand up, he was prodded into a boxcar packed with prisoners, where he stood as the train jostled and jolted, adding new cars and going nowhere. He stood because there was no room to sit. He stood just to avoid the slick fecal slurry that painted the floor. He stood as the train moved east an hour or two at a time. He remained standing as the prisoner cars were parked on a sideline so troop trains could use the single track to move higher priority *Wermacht* soldiers to the western front. Other prisoners drank whatever water they could find during these short waits, but not Billy. Six of his teeth were broken off at the gum line. The blinding pain didn't let him eat or drink, and he couldn't breathe the winter air in through his mouth.

He was nearly dead from dehydration when the train slowed to a stop outside of Gorlitz, unloading Billy and five hundred other Americans into a place known as Stalag 8-A. He didn't remember walking into the camp.

German and American medics worked to clear the broken teeth from his gums. Infection had set in, and with it, fever. Billy was delirious and weak, so the prison dentist decided that he would never remember the agony of root nerves being torn loose so he saved the anesthetic for someone who might really need it. The infection was deep and there was nothing else they could do under the circumstances. They pulled all of his teeth.

There were no false teeth for prisoners of war. Billy was returned to his barracks after two weeks in the infirmary, subsisting on broth. The other prisoners kept him alive by contributing their own rations to make soup. A month later, he would be able to eat soft bread and stewed vegetables. He would need them.

Early in the morning on the tenth of February, all of the American and British prisoners were assembled for roll call. They were divided into groups of three hundred men and marched, at gunpoint, out of the barbed wire main gate and onto the highway. Two by two, they walked west, away from the Russian advance, toward Dresden.

By noon of the following day, Billy's group had marched to the town of Bautzen, where they turned north. They pushed on for two more days before their food ran out. As they passed through village after village, the inhabitants hurled rocks and curses. On the fifteenth of February, the news reached the German captors that Dresden had been annihilated. *Dresden!*

Waves of shock tore through the three-dozen guards and soon they openly talked about killing their prisoners and going home. The only German officer was a young SS Lieutenant. He stood alone and aloof as his men huddled together against the intense winter air, plotting one final act of hopelessness in a lost war.

Billy didn't understand German, but he could plainly see that orders were being barked and arguments were being barked back. The Lieutenant spoke more quietly, then nodded and walked to the edge of the group of prisoners, stopping a few feet from where Billy was sitting.

"Who iss at senior, please?" he asked in broken English. The prisoners stared back at him, dumb. The officer repeated his request more loudly. *"Who iss senior?"*

Billy heard a voice several yards away and turned around to see an American officer in a threadbare green jacket stand up. "Captain Newberry," he called out, "Horace L."

The German lieutenant walked over to him and the two men exchanged salutes. "And your second?" he asked. "Who iss second?"

Captain Newberry motioned for a British officer to stand beside him. "*Leftenant* Wank," he introduced himself, "Bugger U."

The German officer ignored the snickering coming from a small patch of British prisoners. He beckoned the Allied officers to walk with him, and then pointed at two guards, who immediately fell in on either side. They walked a few paces away from the group of resting prisoners. Billy noticed a dozen prison guards take up evenly-spaced positions along the line of POWs. Most of the guards were armed with Mauser bolt-action rifles but some held MP-41 submachine guns at hip level.

He strained to hear what the three officers were talking about. There was a solid sorrow to the German's broken English, but Billy could only make out a few words. He heard something about bombers at night, and something about Dresden.

The German spoke softly, and the British officer repeated everything he said loudly enough to be heard by the prisoners.

"Dresden has been destroyed. A couple of days ago. Bombers."

This news cheered the prisoners immediately. The prison guards quelled the celebrations with their rifle butts.

The American officer called the group to attention, giving the command three times before order was finally restored.

"This is not a goddam football game," he shouted. "Dresden was home to many of these people pointing guns at you now. Stand at ease and don't be stupid."

The German officer spoke again.

The Brit followed with a brief warning to the men to remain absolutely silent, and then said, "The entire city of Dresden is gone."

The German had more to say, and the Brit spoke his next words carefully. "The Nazi guards have voted to kill all of us. Seems he has a bit of a mutiny on his hands. This chap has talked them out of it, for now. He says he made an accommodation with his men."

Captain Newberry asked, "What do you mean, *an accommodation*?"

The German officer spoke in English again. He addressed the two allied officers just loudly enough for Billy to hear.

"Ve liff in impossible times."

The German snapped to attention and saluted, touching the bill of his cap with his fingertips. The American was just beginning to return the salute when the German guards on either side of them each fired a single shot.

Billy watched the two allied officers crumple into the snow. He felt a detached curiosity but no deep concern. His teeth hurt.

Days of marching lay ahead. Despite their agreement to spare the enlisted men, the German guards dealt swiftly with prisoners who fell behind in the march. Their policy was "one warning, one bullet". It was actually more humane than the alternative. The nights were deadly cold. The mornings held more and more of the weak and hopeless firmly frozen to the ground where they had slept the night before.

In early March, Billy found himself walking into another POW camp. He had no idea where he was. It was just another Stalag, cold and indifferent. There was no infirmary here. There was no soup, and precious little bread. Prisoners were brought to Stalag 3-A to die.

The ground was too hard to dig graves, so the bodies of those who surrendered to starvation lay where they fell. The doomed knew Death was eager and many hurried to their chosen place, some in a cold corner of the barracks, some in the frigid open air and rocky soil of a walkway. One at a time, sometimes in pairs, they lay down on the icy ground and slept.

The living pitied the dead, or perhaps it was envy. On the dark, early morning of April 21st, Billy stumbled over an emaciated British sergeant who had died between two barracks an hour earlier. Weak from hunger, Billy could not stop himself from falling face-first into the snow next to the dead soldier.

He lay in the white, cold softness until he was certain nothing was broken, and then carefully rolled onto his side. Barely a foot away, the Brit's face was lighted by the bright moon. The dead man had red hair, but the fat and muscle of his face had wasted away. Billy looked closer and saw *himself* lying there, mummified, forever comfortable and warm in the snow's timeless embrace.

He got angry. He made up his mind he was going to LIVE through this madness. Billy pushed himself up onto his knees and cursed the pain. He would survive the damn Nazis. Wobbly legs slowly lifted him to his feet. He would LIVE through this frozen Hell. He would LIVE through it and go home to Abigail and never, ever leave. Never again!

Billy tried to thank the British Tommie, but his voice only uttered a dry, agonized croak. Weakly, he saluted the corpse and walked around its legs, more carefully this time. By God, he would *live* through this night. Of that much, he was certain.

Two days later, the remaining prisoners awoke to find the guard towers empty and the front gate wide open. Foreign soldiers were arriving in the camp, dressed in green and speaking a language that sounded like German, but different. "*Russians*," Billy said to no one. "*Russians.*"

Liberation brought nothing with it. The Russians had no food to share, no blankets. They walked into the camp searching for Germans to kill. A pair of laughing Russian soldiers had found one of the guards hiding just beyond the edge of the woods outside the Stalag. They dragged him into the assembly area and let his arms go. Billy recognized the German, a boy no older than sixteen. He had seen him manning a guard tower, looking lost in his ill-fitting infantry uniform.

One of the Russians slammed the butt of his machine gun into the young guard's kidney, dropping him to his knees. The small crowd that had gathered to stare at the German pressed forward. The other Russian pulled out his revolver and held it by its barrel. He offered the gun to an American prisoner, a corporal.

"*Oonyestee*," the Russian said. "*Pree tsel i vaat sa vi…*!" He mimed aiming the revolver at the German, and then slapped the gun into the corporal's hand. "*Strel, strel baa* – SHOOT!"

Billy turned from the scene, disgusted, and walked stiffly upright out through the camp gate, past curious soldiers and civilians. In the distance, he could hear a single "pop" as the Russian revolver spat its bullet. Even from a hundred yards away, he could clearly see the expressionless death on the young guard's face.

He walked down the dirt road for several miles until it met a larger, asphalt-covered boulevard. Billy sat down to catch his breath and was promptly arrested by three Russian soldiers who mistook him for a German until they saw his missing teeth and handed him, none too gently, to their medics.

Russian hospital tents were his home for the next month. He managed to scribble three letters during that time, handing each one to a Russian nurse whose mastery of English was suspect and who misunderstood his postal needs. Every letter was put into the garbage.

Germany fell completely by the middle of May 1945. The Russians figured out at last that Billy was speaking an English dialect, so when they joined with British forces they handed Billy over to them. By this time, infection had set in again. The Brits transported Billy to a specialized facility in London.

He tried writing another letter to Abbie, but getting it past the staff was its own kind of war. The infection left him with a sore jaw and swollen, toothless gums. This would have been enough of a speech impediment by itself, but Billy spoke with a rural Mississippi accent, unintelligible to British ears.

So the phrase "I need a pen and some paper so that I can mail a letter home", spoken through a drawl with sore gums to a Briton became, *"Ah nayd a peeyn in zum payupah sosedat ah kin mayaol uh layatuh howum."* Billy never got to send his letter.

In early July, he was finally well enough to repatriate and was transferred onto a troop ship bound for Norfolk, Virginia. During the two-week Atlantic transit, the infection came back to life, this time as staphylococcus spreading into his jaw and threatening his heart and lungs. Half conscious, Billy was put into isolation and the medical staff waited for him to die.

The ship's chief surgeon, Captain Marcus Dunn, had other ideas. Prior to leaving Great Britain, he had obtained a large quantity of a new gram-positive antibiotic from the Radcliff Infirmary in Oxford. They had just developed a technique to mass-produce the drug, called "penicillin". Whether or not the new drug was dangerous was briefly taken into account. The risk was moot since Corporal Dare was going to die without it, so Dr. Dunn decided to start his own clinical trials at sea.

Billy was held in isolation aboard the ship for two full weeks after making port. His infection had cleared up completely. Dr. Dunn came into the ward without a mask one morning and told the surprised patient, "Well, Corporal. It's time for you to go home. Can I get you anything before you're discharged?"

"Yes sir," Billy said through jaws that were still a little stiff. "I need to write a letter to my wife."

"Don't bother, son," the doctor advised. "You'll be home before the letter can get delivered."

Forty-eight hours later, he was wearing a new uniform and signing his discharge paperwork. The duty officer sitting on the other side of a wood desk shoved a small stack of forms in front of Billy.

"Sign here, here, and initial here." The officer pointed at one line and then another. Billy didn't know what he was signing, but he had learned his lesson about asking officers to read the forms to him.

Finally, the officer asked, "Where do you want to go, Corporal?"

"Sir?"

"Where to?" the officer repeated. "Home. Where's home?"

"Passable, Mississippi, sir."

The officer pulled a stiff cardboard form out of a wooden box and on the top line wrote, *"Passable, Miss."* He tore off the onionskin copy and handed the stiff original to Billy.

"Just show this to the bus dispatcher," he said. "Station's at 701 Monticello Avenue. Good luck, son."

And so on Saturday, August 4th, 1945, Billy shouldered his duffel bag and walked toward the Greyhound station, eight miles away. It was a long walk, and he arrived after the last bus of the day had left. He found a comfortable bench and settled in for a long night's wait.

The next morning, just before lunch, Billy boarded the large Greyhound Express Service bus to Meridian, Mississippi. The trip would take eighteen hours, with three stops for passenger comfort and meals. The dispatcher had given Billy a second ticket for the Greyhound Local Direct Service from Meridian to Memphis, with a quick stop in Passable, Mississippi to discharge one passenger.

Three days after walking into the Norfolk bus station, Billy was back in the Northbridge house, standing in front of Abigail, afraid to move. He still wore his khaki trousers and his undershirt. She sat on the edge of her bed, dressed in a simple slip. "The light," she whispered.

Billy couldn't bring himself to turn the light switch off. None of this was real. None of it was happening. If he touched the light switch, the room would turn cold and he would wake up at Stalag 3-A. He knew Abigail wasn't there, not really. She was probably that dead British soldier or the teenage German guard. His heart beat loudly, painfully.

Nausea hit Billy fast and hard and he bolted into the living room, hoping for solitude, ignoring Abbie's objections. Hyram was already there, sitting in the large chair, reading.

"Good evening, William," he said.

"Mister Northbridge." Billy's eyes searched the room for another book. He could try to muddle through the words. The effort would help him fall asleep. The last thing Billy wanted now was conversation.

"Can't sleep, son?"

"No, sir."

Hyram set his book down and pointed to the couch. "That old couch is uncomfortable," he noted, "but nobody will bother you about sleepin' on it." He got to his feet and clicked off his reading lamp.

Billy said nothing. He just settled backwards against the soft couch, more luxury than he had known in years.

Hyram walked to his daughter's room and gently knocked on her door. "Abbie?" he called out just loud enough for her to hear.

"Go away."

Instead, he opened the door and slipped quietly into her room. "Got a minute for your old Dad?"

Abbie slipped a robe over herself and sat on the bed as Hyram pulled a chair over from her vanity. "I don't want to talk," she told him.

"I didn't come here to listen to your little problems, young lady. Dry your tears and pay attention to what I have to say."

Abbie's jaw dropped and the tears disappeared in the shock of hearing her father speak to her like that, especially now, when she needed an understanding shoulder so badly.

"Done bein' all wet and weepy? Good. Some men, like Billy, have simply seen too much. He needs time to sort it out. You're not going to get the old Billy back. He's gone. You may not like the man he's become, but then again, maybe you'll end up with an even better one. You're the wife, Abbie. Whether you get back a husband worth having is up to you at this point. You have to be the anchor. Be strong. Be patient.

Be brave enough for both of you." Done with his speech, Hyram rose from the chair and opened the door to leave. "Oh, yes. Be yourself. He needs that most of all."

Billy awoke just after sunup. He had been snoring, dreaming of snow and people shouting. His dream was a loud one. Loud with truck engines, loud with trains, loud ships, loud bus stations. Then suddenly he was awake and his eyes were open and the Northbridge house was filled with the loud silence of a clock ticking.

He looked around the room. The day's first light washed away the room's shadows and illuminated a pair of bare feet on the floor next to him. They were attached to Abigail. She was sitting in the reading chair, her eyes open and fixed on Billy's face.

Billy croaked, "Good mornin'."

"Same to you," she answered, not moving.

"Have you been there all night?" he asked.

"Uh-huh." Abigail straightened up and quivered in an early morning stretch. "Daddy told me you're feeling lost and you need some time alone, so I shouldn't push at you too hard."

Billy stared at his hands.

She brushed the wrinkles from her skirt and continued, "Well, Mister William Dare, that's not how things work around here, and I'll be damned if I'm ever gonna sleep in any room that doesn't have you in it." She stood and said, "Never again. You can sleep on the couch if you want, but I'm going to be in the chair. You want to sleep in the back seat of the car? I'll be in the front seat. You sleep on the porch, I'll be in the swing."

"You have a swing?" he asked. "When did you get a swing?"

"In April."

"I want to see." They tiptoed out the front door and sat on the wooden porch swing, the chains that hung from the awning creaking as Billy's toes pushed them back and forth.

Abigail reached across the gap between them and caressed the back of his left hand. "You're not wearing your wedding ring," she observed.

"Germans took it."

"How do you like your eggs?" Mrs. Northbridge's voice called out through the screen door.

❧ CHAPTER SIXTEEN ❧

"There are times to wake up the past and times for leaving the past behind."

> Charlotte Montgomery

Billy kept secrets from his wife, but he told Hyram nearly everything. He told him about the capture in the Ardennes, and about the interrogation that had cost him his teeth. He told him about the death march through the German winter, and about the starvation, and about the brutality of the Russian liberators. He tried to tell the story of the teenage German guard, but every time he started, his throat closed up and he felt sick.

Hyram kept secrets from his wife, but he told Abbie nearly everything.

Kennison Meeder heard Billy was back three days after the Greyhound dropped him off. He immediately locked his office and drove straight from Irondale to the Northbridge home, sometimes fast enough to attract official attention. Billy and Abbie were sitting on the porch swing together when Kennison pulled in and hurried out of his car.

"Billy! Billy!" The old man was flushed with excitement. He hadn't realized how much he missed his apprentice until this moment.

A wide grin spread across Billy's face. He stood up, sending the swing gyrating uncomfortably with Abbie still in it. Billy met Kennison at the top of the porch steps. "Mister Meeder," he said.

"You call me *Mister Meeder* again and I'll knock you flat on yer ass... oh, Abbie, hello, sorry, flat on yer *butt*," he corrected himself.

"It's all right, Kennison," she said, "you already said 'ass' and I'm still breathin'."

Kennison grabbed Billy in an earnest bear hug.

"Kennison, you crook," Billy grunted as he hugged his ex-boss and old friend. "God, it's good to see you again!"

"You're too skinny, Bill. Abbie, he's too skinny – do something. Feed this boy!" He stepped around Billy and reached out to shake Abbie's hand. Kennison detected an aging in her face that reached beyond the war years, but she looked happier now than he could remember so he kept his opinions to himself. He gripped Billy's shoulder with one brick-hardened hand and asked what his plans were now that he was a civilian again. He didn't wait for an answer.

"Bill, when can you start? Your old job, your old pay. Plus, I reckon, a ten percent pay raise for each year you were overseas. Lemme see, that's about..." he scratched his head trying to calculate the pay raise, and immediately gave up. "Oh, let's just call it a fifty percent raise."

Billy couldn't stop grinning. "Kennison, that's so generous. I don't know what to say."

"Say 'No'." Abbie's voice was out of place in these delicate negotiations. Both men gaped at her.

Billy laughed at her little joke, "Abbie!"

She was undeterred. "Seventy-five percent. He's got a wife now, Kennison. Responsibilities. Expenses."

Kennison Meeder set his jaw and thought about her demands. "Fifty-five percent," he said. "He still doesn't know how to do arch work."

Abbie got out of the swing and stood directly in front of him, her arms crossed. "I know all about your promise to teach him arch work, Kennison. And I know you've been waiting for a customer who needed an arch, so it's not his fault that you didn't teach him. Seventy percent."

"If you can guarantee that he gets to work on time, then the two of you are worth every penny." He held out his hand to shake on the deal, but Abbie preferred a hug.

Billy started back to work laying brick for Meeder Masonry almost as soon as he could change clothes. Kennison insisted he use the newer "company" truck instead of the old Chevy pickup. It was tax deductible, and counted as an advertising expense because it said "Meeder" and "Masonry" at the top and bottom of a circle painted on both doors. Billy drove the Meeder truck everywhere. His old Chevy sat in the Northbridge driveway, gathering dust.

Living with Abbie's family was frequently difficult and wrought with delicate social obstacles. Laying brick was heavy, sweaty work, and Billy usually came home in the evening covered in body salt, desperate for a bath. With four people in the house, competition for hot water was fierce. The little house only had one bathroom.

Despite her fondness for Billy, Mrs. Northbridge loudly regretted that the boy either took up all the hot water or tainted the delicate olfactory balance of her home. Bathing, however, was not the only challenge.

Abbie enjoyed cooking for the family whenever she could wrestle the kitchen away from her mother. Her meals turned out differently than the same ones cooked by Mrs. Northbridge, but Abbie was still learning.

Although her culinary talents steadily improved, dietary restrictions were imposed after Valentine's Day, 1946. Abbie wanted to try something different and exotic. She had recently seen a magazine article suggesting that the Mayan culture thrived into very old age by eating a diet of fish, maize, pinto beans, and jalapeno peppers. Although there was no recipe, the mixture sounded good enough to try.

She couldn't find jalapeno peppers, so she substituted cayenne, adding a little extra because she had heard how hot jalapenos were. The resulting meal turned out to be unpredictably filling, rendering the family speechless after only two or three forkfuls, unable to eat a single bite more.

"Did you like it?" she asked everybody after dinner was over.

"Oh, yes." "Absolutely." "Yumm."

She was pleased with herself until several hours later, when the first signs of gastric distress made themselves known. Mrs. Northbridge confined herself to her bedroom with the door closed. Abbie heard her mother groaning, and between expressions of pain, the sound of corduroy rubbing against itself.

"What's wrong with mama?" she asked the men, who had retired to the porch swing wearing gloves and winter coats. They giggled like little boys. Hyram made a face and pointed at his belly button. "Migraine, I think she said."

Both men snickered at this, then covered their mouths and laughed. Their faces were portraits of pain. Abbie was certain that they were grimacing every time they laughed and then there was that corduroy sound again, only this time from Hyram's direction. Billy found the noise hilarious. He guffed a little belly laugh and out popped his own corduroy sound. Hyram waved fresh air into his nose, complaining about Billy's manners.

The rest of the evening saw four people with urgent intentions competing for the same bathroom. Doors and windows open wide in desperation, they let a freezing winter wind blow through the house. Mrs. Northbridge got up early the next morning and prepared breakfast herself.

✥

In the middle of March, Abigail woke up to find herself alone in the bed. It wasn't like Billy to let her sleep in on a Saturday. Her mother was banging pans in the kitchen and she could smell ham cooking. Pulling on a robe, she rubbed the sleep from her eyes and offered to help make breakfast.

"Where did Billy go?" Mrs. Northbridge asked.

"I don't know," Abbie answered. "I didn't see him. I just got up."

"His old truck is gone. Can you make toast, please?"

Hyram came in from the garden and brushed the dirt from his cuffs before sitting at the table. Mrs. Northbridge laid a plate of country ham and eggs and toast in front of him and asked, "Where did Billy just take off to?"

He shrugged and kept eating. Abbie's suspicious side woke up and she pressed her father for an answer. "Daddy, didn't he say anything to you before he left?"

"Uh-uh," he said. He shoveled more eggs and toast into his mouth, saving the country ham for last. It was the best part of breakfast.

She was irritated by Hyram's silence. "You *do* know where he went," Abbie accused.

"I can't tell you anything about it," Hyram answered as he ate. "He'll tell you himself when he gets back."

Abbie angrily marched out the front door and perched on the swing, fuming. Two hours later, the old Chevy truck pulled up to the house. Abbie stood and waited for her apology, then watched in disbelief as Billy got out the passenger side, shook hands with the driver and walked into the house. He didn't even look back as his truck drove away without him.

"Where have you been?" she demanded. "Who's that in our truck?"

"Let's go for a drive." Billy paused at the house just long enough to pick up the keys to the "Meeder Masonry" truck.

Hyram smiled at Abbie and nodded his head in approval. Mrs. Northbridge glared at her husband. "What's going on?" she demanded.

"Shhh," he said. "It's a surprise for Abigail."

Billy's mysterious grin was aggravating. Abbie didn't like surprises and wasn't going to endure his teasing in silence. "This is a nice truck," she tried as an icebreaker. If she could get him talking about his truck, she was certain he would talk too much.

"Yup," Billy agreed, grinning and adding nothing she could use. They came to Passable, turned down Main Street and then headed out of town on County Line Road. County Line stopped where Henderson Road began.

"Where are we going?" she asked impatiently. She had only been up Henderson two or three times in her life, but those were enough. There wasn't anything to see here. Henderson crossed a set of railroad tracks, skimmed perilously close to a swamp, and then climbed up a wide knoll known as Henderson Hill.

Just before the road leveled off, it bent sharply to the left. Abbie knew of two people who had run off the road in this turn. They were both drunk at the time, but the county was obliged to put up a guardrail anyway.

She became impatient. "Where's your old truck? Where's the Chevy?"

"Gone," he answered, slowing down and pulling off to the side of the road.

"Gone where?" she demanded. "Why are we stopping? What is all this?"

Billy turned in his seat, his eyes wide and happy and innocent. "This is home," he said. "You're home."

Abbie twisted in her seat and looked around. Old barbed wire and a pair of oak saplings stuck up above an abandoned cow pasture on top of Henderson Hill. There wasn't anything here. There were no power lines. There were no houses. No stores. No people for as far as she could see. There was nothing here at all.

"Home?" Abbie looked again.

"Home," he repeated. "Yours. Mine. Ours. Home. I bought it. We're going to live here."

She had never seen a more beautiful sight. She gasped. "When? How?"

He got out of the truck and walked around to the front bumper. Abbie hurried out of her door and took several long, tentative seconds before joining him.

"You bought this land? How could you afford this with money so tight?"

"It wasn't all that expensive. Anyway, I didn't buy all of Henderson Hill," he said, pointing at a faraway fence post. "That right there is the north corner, and the road here is the west border, down to those trees there," his pointing finger swept north to south.

"You're avoiding the question, William," she said. "How could you afford this?"

"I've been saving – taking on extra work, too. And there was the Army money when I mustered out…"

"Hogwater! Army pay couldn't be enough for all this."

"…and I sold the Chevy…"

"…Oh, no, Billy, not your truck…"

"…and Mister Henderson wanted us to have the place. Did you know that he lost his grandson at Bastogne?"

"Mister Henderson? The banker? G. Henry Henderson?"

"Yeah. He used to raise cattle out here before he bought the bank. He owns all the surrounding land. That's why it's called Henderson Hill," he laughed.

"I never gave much thought to the name," she admitted. "What do you mean, he wanted us to have it?"

"He called me at Meeder's a few weeks after I got back and asked whether I knew his grandson. He was with the 82nd, but I told him that I didn't know him. And then he asked me to go down to his office, so I went."

Billy gestured across the hilltop and continued, "All this was supposed to be passed down to his grandson. Mister Henderson said that he'd heard about my troubles – you know, in Germany – and he wanted to talk to me about the land. He didn't have any heirs and he didn't want the government to get Henderson Hill, so he made me an offer."

"What kind of offer?"

"One-fifty an acre, and keep the name on the map."

Abbie stood up, turning her head this way and that, trying to gauge the size of the parcel. "I don't know about that price. Sounds a little high. I wish you had talked to Daddy first. He would have let us have a few acres right near home for free."

But what she was looking at on Henderson Hill was more than her parents' twenty-or-so acres in the woods. This was new land, independent land. This was *their* land.

"So this is ours? How far back does it go?"

"About half a mile..."

"Mile? Half a *mile*? Billy, how much land did you buy?"

"Two hundred and fifty acres," he said.

"William! No! We'll never be able to pay for this." She did the math in her head. "We'll owe over thirty thousand dollars!" Abigail fought the sudden money panic as she tried to understand why her husband had secretly done something so stupid!

"What?" Billy laughed. "No, no. Abbie... not one hundred and fifty per acre." He brought his face close to hers and whispered, "One dollar and fifty cents an acre. I paid cash. The land is ours."

He waited for her reaction. She snorted once and then started laughing. Billy held her tightly and repeated over and over, "Ours. It's ours. Ours."

"C'mon, I'll show you where the house goes." He held her hand tightly as they sidestepped the fallen barbed wire and cautiously made their way to a pair of young oaks growing about a hundred yards in from the fence line.

He scraped a flat spot in the dirt and sketched a set of interlocking squares with a stick. He explained the floor plan as he went. The kitchen would have windows facing east, to catch the morning sun for breakfast. There would be a dining room, and a family room, and two bedrooms connected by a wide hallway.

Abbie took the stick and drew a second hallway in the back of the house. She sketched a large kitchen, a back porch, and a central fireplace. Billy wiped her drawing area flat with his hand and started over, adding a third bedroom and a pump house. Abbie erased Billy's work and started over, showing him a couple of new ideas. Back and forth they went, building their house on Henderson Hill over and over until they knew for certain what it was going to look like.

❧ CHAPTER SEVENTEEN ❧

"Billy started building the house in early May 1946. Big changes happen when you bring a house into the world."
Charlotte Montgomery

The rains were coming but the house would not wait. Billy bought lumber and nails from the Passable Gin and Mill and laid the foundation himself. He planned each step meticulously, measuring every board twice before letting the saw take a bite or the hammer strike a nail.

The oak beams were too heavy for one man to lift, so Billy hooked up a block and tackle to the base of a young gum tree and used rope to drag each beam into place. The foundation was ready to be lifted in three days.

He was trying to figure out how he was going to raise and level the heavy beams by himself when Kennison Meeder showed up with a volunteer crew of five masons. In two hours, they raised and leveled the foundation three feet off the ground. A few of the men brought their own tools and helped Billy hammer together the weight-bearing walls and nail down a tin roof for protection from the spring and summer rains.

And rain it did! Billy spent every weekend and most nights at Henderson Hill, putting in the wooden floors and laying the stone for the fireplace. Some nights were unusually chilly, but stopping to put on a coat meant losing time so he just shivered as he hammered.

On the first day of June, Billy got sick. The women of the Northbridge house hovered over him and fussed and wouldn't let him go back up to Henderson Hill, no matter how bitterly he complained. It was influenza, Doc Thomas said. But Billy was strong and fought it off and was back on his feet in a week.

He drove back to his unfinished house on the eighth day and discovered someone had trespassed in his absence, picking up loose nails, sweeping the floors and gathering scraps of lumber into a manageable pile. The perpetrator had even set nails into the wall studs and hung up his hammer and saw, freshly oiled.

On the tenth day, Mrs. Northbridge herself got sick. The doctor confirmed what his patient already knew, that she had caught the flu from Billy. Doc Thomas told her not to worry, she'd be on her feet in a week.

In the meantime, she complained and ordered her family about as though they were hotel staff. Her kitchen was turned over to Abbie, but the menu was to be followed strictly. There were to be no excursions into Aztec cuisine.

Mrs. Northbridge had planned for spaghetti on Wednesday evening and therefore Abigail would cook and serve spaghetti. She tried to sit at the table with the rest of the family, but had neither the appetite nor the strength and promptly returned to her bed for the remainder of the night.

The next day, her fever had risen to one hundred and two. Her legs ached, and the pain spread to her back and neck. By morning on the third day, she couldn't move her legs at all. Doc Thomas hurried to the house, but by the time he got there, Mrs. Northbridge had stopped breathing.

Infantile paralysis, he wrote on the death certificate. Polio.

The funeral service was quick and large. Over two hundred people crowded into the tiny Grace Missionary Baptist Church.

Hyram was stone-faced and remained seated as the minister led his swollen congregation in song and prayer. One hour later, the only physical evidence his wife had ever existed was written on a granite marker.

Emma Northbridge, 1901-1946

᧏ CHAPTER EIGHTEEN ᧐

"The house was lit by by candles at night, but candles cost money, so most nights the house stayed happily dark."
Charlotte Montgomery

The new house was hardly more than a shell. It appeared normal enough from the outside, but the interior was doomed to a life as a work in progress. Naked walls waited for Billy to save enough money to afford another sheet of drywall. Closets were postponed until he could afford doors for the rooms. He practically lived in the house, sometimes falling asleep on the bare wood floor and not coming back to Hyram's house until the following night.

Abbie reached her limit in August. She talked Hyram into helping her move a mattress out to Henderson Hill. She had not discussed the move with Billy.

"You'll just be in the way," he said.

"I'll be another set of hands."

"The house isn't ready."

"It's ready enough."

They scrimped on every expense they could live without, and Billy bought lumber or nails or a sheet of drywall every payday. Abbie worked by his side, sometimes steadying boards as he sawed, sometimes carrying tools he needed. Sometimes, her just being there was enough for Billy.

Not for Abigail, though. Summer was almost over and her house needed a garden. She marked off a rough square twenty yards across behind the house. She made the garden ready for seeds by hand, turning the dirt with a hoe and a rake and a shovel, clearing the sandstone bits that peppered the topsoil of Henderson Hill. She could watch it grow from the window over the kitchen sink.

It was late in the season but she planted string beans and purple hull peas anyway. Abbie liked the beanpoles. They weren't hard to make, and once the beans were trained and their vines twisted around the poles, the garden looked busy and strong. She wanted tomatoes and squash and green peppers, but those were summer crops and would have to wait.

Her first garden would have carrots and beets, radishes and lettuce. Each vegetable had its own section, and the garden ripened into a quilt of collards and cauliflower and turnips. Abbie surrounded her patchwork with a hem of field corn, giving the deer a place to stop and nibble and get too nervous to venture farther into the heart of the garden.

While his wife planted spinach, Billy finished the walls and got them ready for gypsum board, installing switches and plugs and electrical wire. None of it worked. There weren't any power lines in this part of the county. Electricity on Henderson Hill was an investment the Passable Power Association hadn't been willing to make, so they didn't put the needed poles and wire and transformers into their annual budget.

Without electricity, water had to be carried into the house by hand. Flushing the toilet took at least two trips to the pump. Dishes were washed in cold water. Hot baths were possible when nights were chilly, but they required a sizeable investment of time and effort. Abbie and Bill didn't dwell on the cold baths but instead spent winter evenings sitting by the fire and reading by its flickering light.

When G. Henry Henderson heard that William and Abigail Dare were still living like "wild beasts", he made his displeasure known far and wide. In October 1946, his bank issued notice on two delinquent mortgages and strangely enough, a week later, both the director and the treasurer of the Power Association resigned.

Kennison Meeder was appointed the new director just in time to take delivery of an anonymous donation of five hundred creosote poles, twenty-four transformers, and fifty miles of copper-coated transmission wire.

The Passable Power Association announced its new Servicemen's Assistance Program on the first day in November. Veterans of World War Two were made eligible for discounted rates on electric power. "Distinguished" veterans, including prior prisoners of war, would enjoy additional benefits. Billy was the county's only distinguished veteran. His house was connected to the power grid at no cost.

For her twenty-third birthday, Abbie got a reading lamp.

Taylor Adams was the youngest staff writer on the news desk of the Meridian Star. He had graduated from high school in 1944 with a solid B+ average, a 4-F draft deferment and dreams of a Pulitzer Prize. Instead, he covered rescues of kittens stuck in drains and local 4-H competitions. If the Nelva Restaurant changed its menu, Taylor Adams had the by-line.

This was not what he had planned, not how he wanted his life and career to turn out. So when he stumbled across a recent article in the Passable County Advocate about a war veteran named Billy Dare who had been honored by the Power Association, he smelled a much larger story. Taylor was overdue for a day off, and since the editor didn't seem to care whether or not he was in the office, he took it upon himself to drive into Passable the next day, Friday.

His first stop was the Passable Power Association. The shake-up in the association's leadership still made people jumpy when strangers came around. The receptionist knew better than to cross the current Director, so she told the young reporter to go ask Kennison Meeder himself. Irondale was just a short half-hour drive away.

Taylor walked into Kennison's office with a pen in one hand and a pad in the other, a pose he sometimes practiced in the mirror. The shock of seeing a Reporter barging into your office, pen and pad at the ready, was supposed to intimidate the witness into telling the truth – every gory detail of it.

"What can you tell me about a man named Billy Dare," he leaned in and made a show of putting the tip of his pen against the paper.

Kennison had been nursing the same Cuban cigar for over an hour and the stench was suffocating. "You did that all wrong, boy," he told Taylor. "You're s'posed to start out sayin' good morning and then ask me how to spell my name." He puffed and waited.

Taylor was embarrassed by this brief dressing-down. So he relaxed and started over. "Good morning, Mister Meeder. I'm Taylor…"

"…Adams," Kennison finished for him. "Yes, I know who you are, and you're looking for Billy Dare, and your editor had no idea that you came all the way out here on your day off."

"You called my boss?"

"I suspect that you want to go back with some kind of story about Billy getting' free electricity or bein' a war hero or some such nonsense." Kennison stubbed out the last inch of his cigar.

Taylor was about to take advantage of the pause and ask a question when the older man continued. "Listen to me, boy. You leave that man alone. Billy never asked for special treatment, 'specially the kind that you're tryin' to give him."

Kennison got up and asked to borrow Taylor's notepad. Reluctantly, the young man handed it across. As notepads went, this one was quite good, bordering on ostentatious. The outside was covered in fine black leather and bore Taylor's initials embossed in gold. Inside, the small pad of yellow paper was held in place by a silver clip.

Kennison turned it over, opened it and closed it, admiring the quality. "Let me guess. A gift from a rich aunt?" He folded it closed and gave it back to Taylor. "Come with me. I want to show you something."

The two men walked out into the parking lot where a large yellow mixing truck sat with its engine idling. "Know what that truck does?" Kennison asked.

"Yeah, it mixes cement."

"Now, you see? That's just one more thing you don't know nothin' about. Son, that truck makes dreams come true. It makes bricks stick together, gives cars a place to park and kids a place to ride their bikes. Everybody's got dreams. Even you, I reckon. Lemme see that notepad one more time."

Taylor handed him the leather bound pad. Kennison clicked his mechanical pencil open and scribbled on the top page, then opened the notebook as wide as it would go and showed what he had written. "Can you read that OK?" he asked. "Is it legible enough for ya?"

LEAVE BILLY DARE ALONE!

He waited for the boy to respond. Taylor nodded and tried to snatch it out of the air as Kennison tossed the notepad into the cement truck's open hopper door, where it would become part of a new Esso pump island in Newton.

Taylor drove his car back to Passable, angry and trembling from his encounter at Irondale. He would have to approach the problem from a different angle.

Driving past the Piggly Wiggly, he got an idea. He pulled in to the grocery store, bought two apples, and asked the checkout girl for directions to the Dare house. It wasn't very imaginative, but it worked and her directions were easy to follow.

Less than ten minutes later, he pulled into the driveway. A woman working in the garden looked up at the sound of his brakes and walked over to meet him.

"Mrs. Dare?" Taylor asked, extending his hand. She shook it, brushing her bangs back with her left hand. When she didn't say anything, he continued, "My name is Taylor Adams. I'm a reporter for the Meridian Star and I want to speak with Mr. Dare about what the Passable Power Association did for him."

Her voice was softer than he expected. He had to listen carefully to every word she spoke. "I'm afraid you have made the trip for nothing, Mr. Adams. My husband is not home at the moment. I don't expect him until after dark."

Taylor excused himself and promised to return at a more convenient time. The nearest motel was in Irondale. That presented too great a risk of running into Kennison Meeder again, so he curled up on the front seat of his car. It was not the first time he had slept there.

At daybreak, Taylor drove back up to the Dare house. Billy was on the porch waiting for him. Taylor extended his hand long before he got within handshake range. "Good morning! I'm Taylor Adams."

"I know who you are. Kennison told me." He made no effort to shake the young man's hand.

Taylor let his arm drop back against his side. "Did he tell you what I wanted to talk about?"

"Yeah. About the PPA hooking up my power for free. He said you were gonna make a stink."

"Hell, sir," Taylor laughed, "I didn't have to drive all the way out here just for that. No sir," he shook his head and cast his eyes up at Billy, "I want a *war story*."

"I haven't got any war stories," Billy said. He turned and went back inside the house, closing the front door.

Taylor knocked on the door in a vain attempt to restart the interview. He waited without hearing anyone coming to the door and then tried again, knocking repeatedly. After five tries, he resorted to raising his voice. "Mr. Dare! I just want to write about what you did in the Army!"

Silence didn't deter Taylor Adams. He knocked again, and then again. And then, the door opened and Abigail stepped out to join him on the porch. "Mister Adams, may I bother you for a second of your time?"

"Of course," he agreed instantly.

"Walk to the garden with me," she said, leading the way around the side of the house. Her vegetable garden was breathtaking, not so much for its size as for the precision and thoroughness it conveyed.

"This is a beautiful garden, Mrs. Dare."

"Thank you. These were called Victory Gardens – oh, and please call me Abbie," her smile was simple and disarming. "Do you know what a victory garden is, Mister Adams? No? They were supposed to provide us with more food than our ration cards allowed. In that regard they failed dismally. Not very many people are ready to do the work, you see. My garden is an obsession. It represents more than mere food. It is the one thing in this life that I can do all by myself. I have a knack for it. I know the secret. Would you like to hear it?"

"Yes. Please," Taylor encouraged her. He wasn't sure where this was taking him, but the beautiful lady standing next to him had his attention and wasn't giving it back.

She paused to inspect a nearby beanpole. "What are you looking for, Mister Adams? A war story or a war hero?"

"I don't see the distinction. I want Bill's story."

"Which one? He was drafted. He left his family alone and never wrote. He stayed away too long. He came home. Is that story you want, mister Adams? Or do you want the story where he surrendered to the enemy without putting up a fight? Maybe you'd like the one where his teeth are pulled without anesthesia because the camp medic thought he was too delirious to remember. Billy has lots of stories, mister Adams."

The soft edge of her voice commanded his silence. Abbie faced him square on and finished.

"William Dare tries to be normal again, every day. He cries in his sleep, but at least he no longer screams. He will not talk about himself to strangers. He believes he is alone in the world. He is wrong. None of us are alone, even when surrounded by strangers. During the war, he survived because people he didn't know gave him food and medicine. He survived, and he came back to me when I needed him most. That man saves my life every day, and I hardly know him at all."

Abbie reached down into the first row of her garden and worried loose a single radish. She brushed the dirt off and handed the red orb to Taylor. "I keep very little of the food that comes out of my garden. It thrives because I give away what grows here. That, mister Adams, is the secret of a successful victory garden."

"I don't understand."

"Few people do. It's simple, really. If you give away your harvest, you will never starve."

Taylor stared at the magnificent garden and suddenly understood. He put the radish in his pocket. "Thank you. *That's* the story I want, Missus Dare."

Taylor wrote and put his byline on the tale of the victory garden, with several photos in the Sunday edition. Abigail and Billy both became war heroes overnight.

Grammison's Electric store had some nearly new appliances that had survived two previous attempts at deep discount sales. John Grammison, the "old man" as he was known, listened carefully as his son outlined a way to leverage the old stock for a half page of advertising.

The next day, Old Man Grammison quietly awarded the Dares a brand "new" all-electric kitchen, while his son made it a point to inform Taylor Adams about the store's generosity.

Taylor arrived with a photographer just before the Grammison's truck showed up. They spent the better part of the afternoon running a fresh set of wires so the stove would work. Then they laid brickwork against the back wall, forming a deep hearth for the "new" Thermidor oven. Grammison's even gave them a brand "new" Philco refrigerator.

The final gift was an electric well pump, replacing the old hand pump. The water line into the house was the wrong size, but after a couple of hours with a professional plumber from Irondale, the kitchen sink finally poured out water. It was rust-colored and gassy at first, but there was great joy in turning a knob and watching water flow out of the spigot. Best of all, the water heater worked!

From start to finish, Grammison's spent three days installing wire and water and brick and appliances in the Dare home. Taylor Adams could only stay an hour, and by the time Grammison's was done, the Meridian Star had lost interest. Old Man Grammison never got his free advertising.

❧ CHAPTER NINETEEN ❧

"Toil and joy consumed Abigail's days. The fall air held onto an early chill and everyone seemed to be talking about the future."

Charlotte Montgomery

Hyram's garden died the day after he lost Abbie's mother. In the spring of 1948, he grew tired of staring out over fallow ground. The back yard needed life.

Billy and Abbie were busy with their new house, so Hyram didn't bother asking them for help. It was a one-man job, anyway. He only had the energy for a small garden – some sweet corn and Roma tomatoes and watermelons. There would be no need for beanpoles since Abigail was growing enough string beans and purple hull peas for both families.

It would have been easy to go overboard, but he knew better. Getting the garden back into shape was hard work. Digging and turning the soil extracted a toll measured in blisters and aching arms. The sun beat down on the back of his neck, but Hyram came away from his small vegetable plot with a sense of peace he hadn't known in more than a year. The garden brought balance back into his life, reminding him he had a purpose.

On Easter Sunday, Brother Stephen was in the middle of the convocation when Hyram opened the door into the Grace Missionary Baptist Church and sat in the back corner. Brother Stephen had blamed himself when Hyram quit coming to services, spending the year after Mrs. Northbridge's eulogy wondering if he had inadvertently given offense.

He excused himself from the pulpit in mid-prayer and walked back to where Hyram sat. The two men shook hands and smiled and meant every word of the unspoken greeting that passed between them. Brother Stephen returned to the front of the church and apologized for not finishing the convocation, but explained that when God answers a prayer, it's rude not pay notice.

ॐॐ

"Abbie! What day is today?" Billy yelled from the bedroom.

She was still drying her hair in an old towel and laughing at the question. "Good Lord, Bill, it's a heck of a time to ask. It's Wednesday."

"No, the date. What's today's date?"

"May," she told him. "The fourteenth, I think. Yeah, that's right, it's the fourteenth...Ohmigod! It's Daddy's *birthday*! What'll we do?"

Billy suggested a quick drive to the old Northbridge house. Abigail insisted on making a pound cake, partly to celebrate Hyram's birthday and partly to apologize for not visiting him as often as they should have. It was still warm when she forced it out of the pan and drizzled orange sauce over the crest. She held it on her lap during the drive to Hyram's.

Abbie got out of the car carrying the heavy cake in both hands. She took one good look at the yard and knew something wasn't right. "Billy," she said, "the yard looks terrible."

It was unlike Hyram to go a single week without mowing. The lawn was overgrown and rough, and sticks littered the base of the trees.

"Maybe his mower is broken," Billy offered.

"A push mower?" Abbie asked.

"Well, let's go ask. Maybe the old man needs some help around the house."

They walked up the brick staircase to the porch. Abbie asked, "When was the last time we were out here?"

"I don't know. Two weeks? I've been kind of busy with the house."

"You're not the only one." She had been Billy's right hand, painting, cleaning tape off windows, and shoveling gravel onto the driveway. There were a thousand things to do every week, and the next week they discovered a thousand new things.

Billy knocked on the door and waited. There was no response. He knocked again and waited again and asked Abbie, "Do you think he's in the bathroom?"

"Just go on in," she said.

"We can't do that. It's not our house."

"It was our house last year," she said, reaching for the doorknob.

Billy called out, "Hyram! It's us and we're comin' in so don't be naked!"

Abbie was still laughing when she pushed the door open and the high sweet aroma of a dead animal rushed out to knock the wind from her last giggle and turn it into a gag.

"Oh, acKGH!" she choked on her own nausea and turned around to get fresh air into her nose. "Oh, God. Billy!"

"Wait here," he said, holding his nose and going into the house to investigate. A few seconds after he went in, he hurried back out onto the porch.

Abbie intercepted him on the run. "Daddy? Is he...?"

"Yeah," Billy coughed and released the grip on his nose. His eyes watered and tears flowed out through both nostrils. "I'm sorry, baby. Hyram's dead."

"No!" Still holding the pound cake, she fought the urge to run inside to see her father. She took one step toward the door and had to struggle to keep from running away. Billy stopped her.

"Don't go in there," he said. "We need to go get Doc Thompson."

Abbie nodded, set the pound cake on the porch and walked to the truck, confused and unsure. She didn't cry during the drive into Passable.

The doctor finished up his only patient, a teenager with a broken ankle, and followed their truck in his own car. He struggled for breath when he stepped into the house, but stayed inside with Hyram for nearly ten minutes.

Abbie was sitting on the brick steps cradling her chin in both hands when the front door rattled open and Doc Thompson walked onto the porch. "Abbie, I'm sorry. It looks like Hyram's heart gave out. There's a half-full glass of water on the lamp table and an empty Alka-Seltzer wrapper, and his clothes are filthy. From what I can tell, he was working in his garden and thought he had indigestion. My guess is that he's been gone for about a week."

Billy asked about the odor. Doc Thompson responded, "I opened a few windows, but that house won't likely be fit for people for quite a while."

"What do we do now?" Abbie asked.

"I called constable Mitzner while I was inside," he said. "He called the Passable Sheriff's office. They'll be here any minute."

The sheriff's deputy pulled into the driveway, followed thirty seconds later by an ambulance from Passable Country General. The deputy was new, anxiously taking statements from Doc Thompson, Billy and Abigail, one at a time and out of earshot of one another.

Neither Billy nor Abigail knew where they wanted the remains sent, so they took the ambulance driver's recommendation and followed him to Myer Chapel Funeral Home, the closest one. Abbie arranged for a short memorial at Grace Missionary Baptist in three days' time, followed by a simple burial next to Mrs. Northbridge. They finished their business with Myer Chapel and drove straight home without talking.

The thick odor of death from the Northbridge house clung to their pants and shirts. They bathed and put their clothes in paper bags. They briefly debated whether to wash the clothes or burn them.

The next morning, Billy returned to the Northbridge home by himself to close up the windows and disinfect the air, stopping in Passable to buy three cans of Lysol. As he paid, several people he knew walked by and said "Hi, Bill," or "Nice day."

Later, they would remark to one another that Billy Dare seemed sullen that afternoon. Some would say he was rude.

⚘ CHAPTER TWENTY ⚘

"The house wasn't fit for visitors. It needed a finishing touch."
Charlotte Montgomery

In their second year on Henderson Hill, Abbie asked Billy to make some changes. First of all, she wanted a little privacy. "That bedroom door," she complained one morning over breakfast, "doesn't actually have a door in it, William. As a matter of fact, the kitchen could use a door or two as well."

"Oh," he said. "I thought I'd done real good with the house, considerin' that I built it myself."

"Don't get like that with me, William Dare. I didn't ask you to tear it down and start over. I'd just like a few doors."

"OK, fair enough. I think Short's down in Irondale has some doors."

Short's Building Supply had doors, all right. Anticipating a renaissance of French Creole architecture in Passable County, Papa Short had overruled his sons and ordered half a dozen glass-paned doors. Up until the moment the Dares walked into his store, he thought he'd have to remove the glass and sell the panes as window replacements. Instead, he smiled and waved goodbye as the couple drove off with five French doors in the back of Meeder's truck.

One door was mounted at the kitchen entrance, separating it from the dining room. This actually made the dining room look larger, and cut down on the smoke that occasionally drifted through the house when Billy tried to show off his meager skills as a cook.

French doors were hung on the main bedroom and the back bedroom, giving separation from the hallway but doing absolutely nothing to enhance privacy. Abbie wouldn't hear of returning the doors to Short's and hung white curtains over the glass, instead.

The final two doors were a matched pair designed to be hung side-by-side. Billy had picked them out quietly, without telling Abbie what he was planning. By nightfall, the twin doors sat in the hallway by themselves, leaning against the wall opposite the entrance to the living room.

"Billy," she called out, "You bought one door too many!"

He peered around the opening into the hall and winked. "Nope. Those are special."

"What are they for?"

"Something special," he repeated teasingly.

"William…" her voice carried a warning tone.

"OK, OK," he gave in. "These two go together to make a double door. I'm going to put 'em between the living room and the hallway."

Abbie stared at the open doorway, put her hands on her hips and squared off at Billy. "The opening is too small. Those doors are way too wide. What were you thinking?"

"I was thinking the entire wall will have to be torn out and reframed for the doors, then we put up new gypsum and repaint. Piece of cake."

Abbie focused on the first part. "Torn out? How does one go about doing that?"

"Well, there's the right way and…" he reached into his toolbox and pulled out two hammers. "…then there's the fun way."

Abbie took one of the hammers and flexed it threateningly in the general direction of Billy's head. "Where do I start?" she asked.

Billy produced a black crayon and traced a circle in the middle of the wall. Then he stepped back and gestured with an open hand toward the fresh target.

Abbie didn't wait to be told. She grinned and swung and let her hammer pound into the wall with all the fury she could bring to bear, punching a hole in the fresh white gypsum board the size of a half dollar. "You gotta be kidding. This is going to take awhile," she said.

Abbie and Billy took turns bashing the outer wall and peeling the remains from the oak studs. Then she got busy sweeping up the floor while Billy used the claw of his hammer to pull the nails that had held the drywall in place. An hour later, the skeleton of the living room wall lay exposed to the elements.

For the rest of the day and into the night, Billy showed her how to pry nails out of a board, peeling wood studs away from their headers. One after the other, boards fell to her hammer and lay on the floor.

Billy taught her to measure with a folding ruler, marking and sawing the old doorway until they finally had a box frame precisely the right size to embrace the double doors. He showed her how to mark the doorframe for the hinges, then watched her hands guide the razor-sharp chisel with light hammer taps, stripping away thin wafers of wood until at last, the first hinge slid tightly into place in her newly-cut recess.

Again and again, Abbie shaved and chipped away at the wood, coaxing the hinges into their snug mortises, mating the doors to the frame with an intimacy she had never imagined possible.

Finished at last, Abbie slumped breathlessly to the hallway floor and pulled herself next to Billy, resting her chin on his shoulder. The doors hung lonesome on the wall's wooden skeleton, but Abbie's eyes saw a finished hallway, covered in gypsum and painted white, and in the middle, double French doors!

The doors held thirty panes of glass that formed a window between the hallway and the living room – fifty pounds of wood and paint and brass. But to Abbie, they were a work of art worth more at this moment than the entire house, more than all of Henderson Hill. No longer mere doors between rooms, they were a gateway into the soul of her home.

She leaned against Billy and let her mouth search his face, his hands, and his shoulders. Without argument, without words of any sort, he followed her into the bedroom. They left the door brazenly open and surrendered to the nightfall.

❧ CHAPTER TWENTY-ONE ❧

"Life on Henderson Hill had a flavor of sameness about it, even as the rest of the world stumbled and lurched over new ground. "
                                        Charlotte Montgomery

Henderson Hill was racing the world to become modern. In 1948, Southern Bell ran telephone wires to the Dare house, and suddenly their living room was connected to fifty million other living rooms around the world.

Bill and Abbie took turns lifting the handset and listening to the off-hook signal. As much fun as this was, neither of them could think of anyone they wanted to talk to, so they went to bed early. There were garden chores to be done in the morning. Summer vegetables had to be planted. Tomatoes and squash and bell peppers brought the garden alive in a blaze of color.

The bugs had too much fun with the squash that year, so in 1949 Abbie sprayed the whole garden with DDT.

In 1952, the bugs were back. DDT was being blamed for all sorts of evil, so Abigail changed tactics and surrounded the squash patch with marigolds. Theoretically, the bugs would eat the first flower they came across and get sick. It worked.

In 1953, the bugs went wherever bugs go when they eat bug poison and Abbie doubled the size of her garden. She added sweet corn and watermelon. Cucumbers, small and large, swelled on the vine and were picked and pickled. Cantaloupes flowered, sprouted and lay on the sun-drenched ground waiting patiently for Abbie to make her rounds and turn them over.

The beans stayed in the section oddly called "the bean patch." Tomatoes always grew best outside the shade of the house, so she hammered together enough trestles to grow several bushels of the sweet red fruit each year.

In 1954, she added potatoes and onions. The onions were small but sweet, earning a coveted place in the moist soil beside the kitchen wall. The potato crop rotted. The soil was good, though, so she used it strictly for radishes and other winter crops.

Billy's days were spent laying brick with Kennison Meeder. The masonry business was doing quite well. By 1955, Billy owned his own truck and with some help from G. Henry Henderson's bank, purchased a used Ford tractor and spent weekends mowing down the wild pastures that surrounded the Dare house.

Television came to Henderson Hill in 1958. Billy brought home a large, heavy wood box and plugged it into the wall socket. The darkened glass front crackled with static. Billy adjusted the tuning knob through all thirteen channels, finding nothing but formless snow. He unplugged the television and put it on the back porch, where it was used as a table.

Kennison Meeder had taken on a large amount of debt so that Meeder Masonry could modernize its operations and double their payroll. He didn't expect to die of pneumonia in 1961.

Billy took over the business and paid on Meeder's debts until the old man's estate was solvent. He showed himself to be a good businessman, and a man who knew how to repay kindness. As much as the people of Passable liked Kennsion, they loved Billy Dare like he was their own son.

Year after year, Abbie's garden marched forward to a slow, steady drumbeat. She planted and nurtured, embracing the labor that made a harvest possible. In the terrible heat of the Mississippi summer, she struggled on her hands and knees, ripping weeds out of the ground to make room for seedless melons, strawberries, and cantaloupes.

She added garlic in 1970, tending to the tiny plants at daybreak, before the sun became unbearable. The garden grew in size and diversity, yielding more fresh food for the kitchens of Passable. Abigail spent her days in the garden, her hands calloused and blistered by the business of growing.

By 1972, Billy's company had eighteen employees and more work than it could handle. He left for the office at seven o'clock every morning, and every night he would return to Henderson Hill and a quiet evening at home with his Abbie.

Billy came home early one afternoon in June. He kept to himself over dinner, ignoring her attempts to start a conversation. Something about his silence raised her hackles.

She cleared the dishes and gave them a quick swipe, and then marched into the living room and demanded he tell her what was bothering him so much that he couldn't even carry on civilized chitchat at the dinner table.

"Do you remember Howard Germany?" he asked.

"Of course," she answered, "he used to teach at Passable."

"Not any more. He called me today. He wants us to meet with Tom Brighton tomorrow night. Dinner."

"Never heard of him. How's Howard?"

"He's fine and you're not listening. We're having dinner with Dr. Brighton tomorrow night."

"And why would this *doctor* want us as dinner guests?"

"He's the President of Passable Community College. They want to discuss paying me to teach a couple of classes on bricklaying."

"Billy, honey, that's great! But you don't need to meet with the President for that. That sort of job would probably only rate lunch with an Assistant Dean. There's something you're not telling me."

"Maybe," he admitted, "but I don't want to jinx it. For now, we're just having dinner."

Abbie shook her head. "I can't go," she said.

"Why not?"

"Nothing to wear."

"Good thing I'm home early, then." He checked his watch. "Belk's is open 'til seven."

She raced him to the car at a fast walk, excited about the drive into Passable and full of questions about the work at PCC. Billy wouldn't talk about the "high fancy dinner," as Abbie called it. She maneuvered the conversation to other, more important topics – what color her dress should be, how fancy, how expensive. And of course, shoes!

They had barely pulled into the parking space and shut down the motor when Billy put his hand on her shoulder. "I don't know whether it will make any difference, dress-wise," he said, "but I ought to tell you that the dinner isn't a job interview."

"I thought you said that they wanted to talk to you about a job."

"That much is true, but the fact is…well, I already accepted their offer."

"William Dare!" she snapped. "Why didn't you say something?"

"I'm sorry. I really should have checked with you before I accepted, but my mouth just suddenly said 'Yes' and then they were shaking my hand…"

Abbie fixed him with a sideways glare. "What do you mean 'they'? You said Howard Germany offered you a job teaching a couple of classes."

"Well, not exactly…"

"William!"

"They offered me the department," he admitted. "Their new Industrial Arts Department."

"Doing what?"

"Bricklaying, at first. And then carpentry, welding, air conditioning…"

"You can't teach all that. You've never even welded."

"I know," he said, "I'll have to find people to fill those positions."

She nodded and sat pensively, looking off into the distance. "William, you're not going to have the time to teach and run a business, as well."

He nodded. "We'll have to get used to some changes."

"How much can I spend on the dress?"

Billy followed her down one aisle after another as she touched and examined every item of clothing in Belk's. By seven o'clock, she had picked out a pleated navy blue cotton evening dress. It was flattering and demure at the same time, befitting a woman going on fifty years' of age. Abbie really liked the dress, but she whispered to Billy that the price tag was too bold and she'd still need shoes. It was just too expensive.

He took the dress from her arms and kissed her on the cheek. "I like this dress," he said. "It'll look real nice on you. Now go get some shoes before they close."

Abbie scurried off and immersed herself in a sea of burgundy sandals, blue slingbacks, black open toes, and high heels. This was a decision not to be made lightly. Each shoe had to be evaluated on its own merits, measuring one against the other on the basis of texture, heel height, side support, sharpness of the toe, and presence of shiny buckles and baubles.

The social impact of the shoe had to be weighed just as carefully. Was it dressy enough? Was it too dressy? Was it enough shoe for the occasion, or did it hint too heavily at plans for the opera later? Was the style popular? Would she be seen as a Wearer of Inappropriate Shoes?

All these elements were conspiring to test Abbie's judgment. Finally, she found a pair of rather unremarkable patent leather open-toed dress shoes with medium-height heels. She turned them over and over, wishing that the color were a trifle closer to that of the dress. She had almost decided on black as an acceptable color when a well-dressed lady in her mid-forties stopped beside her and spoke.

"Hi, sweetie! New shoes?"

Abigail looked up from her footwear analysis and thought for a second she recognized the woman. The lady had mistaken her for someone else and was standing a few inches too close. Seeing no point in rudeness, Abbie said, "Hi. Yes, and I'm having a lot of trouble selecting the right ones."

"Those seem nice. And black goes with everything." She added that she had seen a belt that would match, and perhaps a handbag, as well. Abbie couldn't concentrate on what the woman was saying. The strangeness of this conversation was putting her off balance, as though she were on the edge of déjà vu.

And just as suddenly as she appeared, she noted how late it was, waved "Goodbye" and left. Abigail watched her until the woman was out the front door and out of view. She was dizzy and could taste her stomach. She thought she might lose dinner right there in the shoe department, but Billy startled her back to reality.

"It's getting late. Are you going to buy those?"

She saw that she was holding a shoe and slowly remembered that they were the right color, but the wrong size. "I have to try on a pair," she said.

"I'll round up a salesgirl for you. What did Sally want?"

"Who?"

"Sally," he repeated. "What did she want?"

"Sally who?"

"Don't be funny," he said.

"What are you talking about?"

"Sally Willis, the woman you were just talking to."

"Oh, I haven't seen Sally Willis in weeks."

A salesgirl came up just then and helped her find a pair of shoes in the color she liked. They paid and apologized to the evening manager for having to unlock the front door to let them out. Abbie had her new dress and new shoes and a matching belt, and she was happier than she had been in months.

❦

Billy asked himself whether he might have misidentified Sally, but was pretty sure he knew her face. Besides, Abbie had told him about running into her just a few days ago. She had lied to him and he didn't know why.

As lies went, it was a small transgression, by itself unworthy of serious consideration. But he couldn't forget it. Sometimes, late at night, the lie would float to the surface and make him aware Abbie was different. She had changed.

❧ CHAPTER TWENTY-TWO ❧

"Complete strangers talked to her like they were old friends. At first, it was funny. "
                                                Charlotte Montgomery

Saturday was grocery day and Abbie's weekly opportunity to have lunch with Billy at Breen's Rexall. She was more than an hour late. She never used to be late, but in the last year or so time just seemed to be farther away than she could reach. Billy was already seated at the long counter, nibbling on a plate of fries when she came around the magazine shelf, apologizing.

"I can't believe how late I am. I don't know where the day went."

"You're here. That's good enough for me."

Billy was like that, always forgiving when she did him wrong, always forgetting when she borrowed a dollar or two off his dresser. And in the two years since the incident in Belk's, he always had a reasonable explanation for why unfamiliar faces would say 'hello' to Abbie, as though they expected her to stop and carry on a conversation.

Being late was understandable. Christmas was a week away, and the roads and stores were crowded.

"Even the waitress is slow today," Abbie observed.

"No, I already ordered us a couple of hamburgers, to save some time."

"Have I become that predictable?" she asked.

Billy didn't have to answer. The waitress set their plates down and double-checked Abbie's order. "Burger, well done, mustard, mayo, no ketchup, no onions," she said.

Abigail was too hungry to disagree. Besides, the burger was exactly the way she liked it. She was in the middle of her second bite when Walter Hibbens strolled in with his wife, Marlene, and their twelve-year old twins.

Walter slapped Billy on the back. "How's it hangin', Bill?" he asked. Marlene pinched her husband on his arm \\and chided him for the crude greeting.

Bill turned around and greeted the newcomers. "How do, Walt? Marlene, you're lookin' good."

"Bill," she replied with a wide smile. "Oh, Abbie, happy late birthday, sugar!"

Abigail lit up on seeing Marlene. They weren't best friends, but Marlene had spent many hours gossiping in Abbie's garden. "Leenie!" she declared, "What're you and Walt doin' in town?"

"A little early Christmas shopping. Just tryin' to get it out of the way before You-Know-Who slides down the chimney," she tried to be sly, although for most boys as old as her twins, the Santa cat was well out of the bag.

"Can't be too careful," Abbie agreed, turning her attention to the two boys. "Well isn't this something," she said, holding out her hand. "Twins!"

Marlene giggled and echoed, "Twins. Yep."

"Now, Mar, as I remember it, *your* boys are twins, aren't they? And about this age, too." She beamed at the pair and then looked around for their parents. She slowly became aware that these two were with Marlene and Walter. "Oh, are you guys spending time with…"

The memory of who the children were came flooding back with sickening waves of embarrassment. In the distance, Abbie heard Marlene laughing light-heartedly at the gaffe.

Billy saw beyond the blush on his wife's cheeks. There was dread hidden in her eyes.

They finished up lunch without eating another bite, paid the check and started walking toward the Piggly Wiggly. Abbie stopped outside the grocery store and refused to go in.

"I can't," she said, "I don't really need anything and I don't feel much like shopping today and there's so much to do at home." She fidgeted with her purse and begged Billy to just drive her back to Henderson Hill.

On the drive back, she didn't talk at all. She just leaned her head against the passenger window. The cold safety glass felt good on her forehead.

She stopped talking about her problem recognizing familiar faces, hoping her memory would get better. It didn't. Her occasional bouts with forgetfulness became a gossip point around Passable. Friends stopped coming around to Henderson Hill. Old friends stopped talking to Abbie completely.

The protective seclusion she enjoyed at home gave her time to recover from the previous winter's storm of strange faces. Spring came and brought a new planting season. Abbie had saved her spare change all year and now was the time to take the half-full coffee can from the kitchen, count her coins and buy seed.

On Saturday morning, she left Billy in bed, asleep, and drove the car to the county cooperative, carrying the same wrinkled shopping list that had worked so well for previous years' gardens. She needed a little bit of sweet corn, and bought enough field corn to plant around the outside of the garden for the deer to nibble on. Lettuce seeds, purple hull peas, and string beans were all carefully selected and weighed. Tomatoes, of course, and bell peppers, and melons, squash, and cucumber seeds were picked out, bagged and labeled.

Abbie paid with cash, dollar bills and quarters mostly. She insisted on counting out the money, laying the coins to one side and smoothing out the crumpled bills as best she could. The transaction finally complete, Abbie smiled at the impatient girl behind the cash register and hefted the box full of seed bags onto one hip.

The co-op was busy that morning, its parking lot crowded. Abigail stood at the doorway and looked for her car. She remembered clearly parking it in front of the customer entrance, but instead of her brown Buick the parking spot held a new Ford four-door.

Confused at first, she figured perhaps she hadn't parked the car where she thought. She walked the parking lot, going from car to car, but hers was nowhere to be seen. "Oh, of *course*," she muttered, suddenly remembered parking near the garden shop, up the hill a short distance from the co-op doorway.

The box of seeds felt heavier as Abbie trudged up the gravel hill. When she got to the top and turned into the garden center parking lot, she saw that neither of the cars parked there was hers.

She grappled with the obvious conclusion. Her car had been stolen.

Stolen! Billy would be furious. He had repeatedly warned her about leaving the keys dangling in the ignition, but Abbie had always felt perfectly safe in Passable, until now. She caught her breath and steeled her spine for the phone call she would have to make to the Sheriff's office.

She walked back downhill to the co-op door and pushed on it, nearly smashing her nose against the glass when the door refused to open. She pushed again, then pulled, but the door was firmly locked. The lights inside were turned off, too.

Abbie looked for the business hours on the door. "Saturday – CLOSED," said the sign. *"That can't be. I was just here,"* she said to herself. She backed up two steps and read the door again. Above the hours, painted in white, were the words "Omega Insurance".

Abbie felt the ground beneath her suddenly drop away. This was wrong! It was supposed to be the Passable

Cooperative. Her box of seeds felt ten pounds heavier. If this wasn't the co-op, she thought, then where exactly WAS the co-op?

She remembered walking uphill to the garden shop, so she reasoned that the co-op must be downhill. She had simply missed the fact that part of the co-op building was being used for Omega Insurance's office. That had to be the reason. Downhill, then, must the right direction. At the bottom of the hill, Abbie turned left.

The Sheriff's office called Billy at home two hours later and sent a patrol unit to bring him to the county courthouse. Abbie was sitting at a gray metal desk, trying to fill out a stolen vehicle complaint. Sheriff Metcalf intercepted Billy before he could reach his wife. "William, we need to talk." The two men slipped into a vacant side office and closed the door for privacy.

"We found Abigail wandering in a bad neighborhood. She was disoriented and lost."

"Where…"

"It doesn't matter where, nothing happened to her," he reassured Billy. "She claimed she couldn't find the co-op, and she was carrying an empty cardboard box. She told my deputy her car had been stolen."

"Stolen? The car was stolen?"

"Relax, no. The deputy drove her to the co-op and she found it right where she'd parked it," he added. "But she swore somebody *had* stolen it, even if they did bring it back."

"I don't understand," Billy said. "What's going on?"

"At first, he suspected your wife had been drinking." The Sheriff lowered his voice. "But before he could run a field test, Deputy Peterson saw something that told him she wasn't drunk. He's pretty good at his job when it comes to DUI. He didn't arrest her. Here, take this," he said as he handed a small card to Billy.

"What's this? Her driver's license?"

"I took it away, but there's no law to back me up on that, so I'm givin' it to you. Give it back to her if you absolutely have to, but if we see her driving in town I'll find some reason to revoke it."

Sheriff Metcalf started to open the door, but paused and said, "You have to get her to a doctor, Bill. Soon. Go on, now. Take her home."

Abbie saw Billy's shadow fall over the table from behind her. She recognized his profile immediately. The solid familiarity of her husband by her side washed away the terror of being lost. She felt like crying. She felt like laughing.

For the next few months, Abigail stayed close to home. Passable had become full of stares and hoarse whispers and the constant threat of changing storefronts and brand new streets. She spent the summer nursing her garden in the cool hours of the morning. When the heat of the Mississippi day bore down, Abbie would open the doors and windows throughout the house and sit in the hallway, napping in the slight breeze.

August brought a brutal stillness to the air on Henderson Hill. The nights were too warm to sleep, so Abbie fought back with a cool bath before bedtime. She set her watch down beside the sink and slid into the tub. A half hour of soaking made the muggy night air more bearable. Had it been a half hour? There was a change in the air she couldn't quite identify. Had she fallen asleep?

Abbie stepped out of the tub and pulled the drain plug. She ran the towel over her hair first, then her arms. She reached over beside the sink to check the time, but her watch was gone.

A quick search of the sink and the cabinet failed to produce her watch. She searched the floor and the tub and under the toilet. She even checked her arms, just in case she had put it back on and forgotten about it. She searched her sock drawer, the jewelry box and every pair of jeans in the dirty hamper. An hour later, tired and half-dressed, Abbie opened the refrigerator and pulled out a carton of milk. She froze in mid-memory as the old Bulova fell off the butter dish, slipped through the wire shelf and clinked to the floor at her feet.

There was drought that year. Abbie worked hard to keep the garden alive. Summer dawns were cool and deceptively pleasant, but within hours the sky changed its mind, focusing white heat that blistered the back of her neck as she worked the dry topsoil. In a matter of weeks, the clear skies and sunburned dirt had sapped the life from her beans and tomatoes. Her sweet corn ripened early and was taken by worms.

Abbie worked her fingers into the dry clay, salvaging the few cucumber roots that still held life. Two inches deeper and the soil hardened into a brittle sandstone layer that fingernails couldn't penetrate. She reached down beside her knee and felt around for the familiar handle to her trowel. It wasn't there.

Squatting on her knees, she rocked back and looked on the ground around her legs, where she had laid it down. It still wasn't there.

"Oh, no," she said. "Not again."

Sweat stinging her eyes, she stood and turned first in one direction, then the other. Nothing at her feet. Nothing in her pockets. She checked the ground at her feet again. *"No!"* she grunted.

Her aggravation built steadily. In her memory, Abbie could almost feel the smooth tin handle of the little digging tool. *"Maybe I left it on the back steps,"* she thought, starting back toward the house. It made no sense to her why the trowel should be fifty yards away from the spot where she had been digging, but the house was cooler than the garden and would be a much more comfortable place to start searching.

Billy had spent the entire morning writing lesson plans, but the tedium of paperwork reached a crescendo by noon and forced him from his desk at the college. The drive home was short. There was no hint of trouble until he walked through the front door.

The drawers had all been pulled out of the console table and lay face down in the hallway, their contents spilling out onto the floor. He stepped carefully into the bedroom, avoiding half-burned candles and old ballpoint pens strewn in his path.

His bureau was untouched but the rest of the room had been turned upside down. All of Abbie's jewelry had been dumped on the bed, along with the contents of two of her dresser drawers.

"Abbie?" he called out. He heard sounds coming from the far end of the house, a metallic rattling that told him someone was in the kitchen. Then a loud *crash* as handfuls of silverware clattered to the floor, followed by Abbie's voice screaming curses.

"Abbie!" he shouted, running headlong through the hallway. As he passed through the living room, he slowed up. Books were randomly spilled about the floor and every drawer on every piece of furniture had been pulled out.

Cautiously, Bill stuck his head through the kitchen door. All of the cupboards were open, and can after can of store-bought vegetables and chili and tuna had been pulled out and set in the sink. The refrigerator was open wide. Flatware had been hauled out of its drawer and thrown down against the linoleum. Abbie sat in the middle of the kitchen floor, her face slick with sweat and tears, quietly muttering, "Damn, damn, damn."

Billy knelt beside her and wiped her face with a clean paper towel.

"Oh, I'm so sorry, so sorry," she apologized over and over, "I can't find it."

"Find what, sweetie?" he asked.

"It was on the back porch, I think. And then I remembered putting it in the hallway," she pointed toward the front of the house. "But it's not there, now and I don't know where it is."

"What's that?" he asked again. "What are you looking for?"

"It's a...thing. You know, one of those – *things*," her eyes flicked across the floor, searching. "I can't quite remember what it's called."

"What kind of thing, sweetheart?" Billy held her hand and tried to calm the panic he saw building in her eyes.

"Oh, I, oh!" she whimpered. "Oh, I have no idea what I'm looking for...DAMN!" Abbie screamed, kicking a drawer full of cooking implements as hard as she could, sending it across the kitchen where it collided with the trash can, showering the floor with metallic clinks and rattles.

"Damn," she said more quietly. Abbie buried her face in Billy's chest. Her tensions melted into heaving sobs. "Oh, damn it all."

Billy held her until she stopped crying and then cleaned her up for the ride to Doc Thompson's.

✎ CHAPTER TWENTY-THREE ❧

"Billy died a little, day by day, watching Abbie change and knowing he couldn't do a thing to stop it."
Charlotte Montgomery

"Billeee!" Her voice stabbed through the darkness and pulled Billy out of a fitful sleep. "Billy, I can't find it. Where did you put it?"

It took a few seconds for his eyes to adjust to the dim pre-dawn light. He rolled over and watched patiently as Abbie scoured through her dresser in a panic. Once more, she had lost "it", and once more, Billy would pay the price in lost sleep.

"Billy, it's gone," she complained, "where did you put it?"

This had become the pattern his life would follow. He never wanted it this way, but he loved the girl as deeply now as he had when she was seventeen. Billy kept telling himself she was just having trouble adjusting to menopause, that she would work through it.

He turned on the radio and listened to the NPR reporter drone on about how fabulous the Bicentennial celebration was going to be tonight. New York City would be ablaze with fireworks. Far overhead, a small airplane engine hummed across the morning sky. Everybody, it seemed, was going somewhere. The irony wasn't wasted on Billy. Abbie was moving around enough for both of them as her search took her deeper into the hallway, deeper into madness.

She would never find "it", not today in any event. Her compulsion to search would not fade for hours. She would empty every drawer in the hallway. She would rummage through the cabinets and silverware drawers in the kitchen, again and again.

Billy knew the search would be fruitless. "It" didn't exist. "It" was vague, taunting and shapeless. "It" would remain just out of reach, like a well-known name you can't quite recall.

He peeked into the medicine bottle and counted five tiny pills. This was the last of his Librium supply, prescribed over a year earlier by Doc Thompson. They were supposed to help Abbie get through her episodes. She didn't trust pills, so Billy would crush the tablets and mix them in with a little Pepsi. Librium wasn't a cure, but it made her compulsive searching bouts more tolerable.

When these five tablets were gone, there wouldn't be any more. The previous winter, Doc Thompson had broken his leg slipping on a patch of black ice while getting out of his car. The old doctor declined an overnight stay at Passable General, preferring the safe comfort of his own home.

Doc Thompson was in the habit of reading one or two passages from the Bible every night, but this one particular evening, the crack in his leg released a fat embolus into his blood stream. When it reached the old, delicate veins in his head, Doc Thompson met Jesus.

His practice was taken over by Natalie Baugham, a young doctor with a shiny new license who didn't believe in anti-psychotic medications. Billy told himself she would change her mind over time, but the five pills in the bottom of the bottle added to the urgency.

"Missus Baugham, my wife *needs* those pills," he pleaded. Firm and professional, the young woman reminded Billy she preferred to be called "Doctor" instead of "Missus", adding that she was disinclined to renew the Librium prescription.

"Mr. Dare, you're only delaying the inevitable," she told him. Abbie's future lay in the round-the-clock care only a good nursing home could provide. Billy knew she was right. But Abbie – his Abbie – had lived under the same roof with him as long he could remember. He'd just try to use a little less of the Librium each time.

Reducing the dosage of the calming drug had the opposite effect than what he had wanted. Her searching episodes became more frequent. Billy tried ignoring them, but he still had to deal with her moody eruptions that quickly turned into fits of temper. These were uncontrollable, bordering on violent.

What remained of the Librium was gone within two weeks. Abbie required gradually increasing attention until, by the middle of summer, Billy couldn't leave her alone for an entire day without continually worrying. Frequently, he would drive home over the lunch hour just to check on her.

His job at the college made demands on Billy's time that he couldn't meet. Having missed three classes in a row, he was summoned to a meeting with the President. The cold practicality of the situation was laid out for him.

His position at Passable Community College would depend on his ability to stick to a class schedule, even if it was merely summer school. Faced with the prospect of losing everything, he finally saw Dr. Baugham was right. She had been right all along.

Billy thought the hardest day of his life was Wednesday, July 28th, 1976. That afternoon, he signed committal papers in the Passable County courthouse. His medical insurance would cover most of the cost, so before going home he made arrangements at Regency Nursing Center ("Community Living for the Elderly Ill"). The paperwork was a blurred cascade of legal language, initials, and signatures.

And finally, with a weak handshake, it was done. Billy returned to his car and started the engine. Drowning in guilt over what he had just done, he told himself he had been pushed to the limit. There was nowhere else he could turn. He didn't believe his own excuses. Billy shut off the car and sat in the hot parking lot and grieved.

The hardest part of the hardest day of his life lay ahead. Billy had no idea how he would do it, but he had to tell his wife she was losing her mind.

And then, he'd have to persuade her to voluntarily leave Henderson Hill. Leave her garden. Leave her glass French doors. He didn't know how she would react. In spite of nearly thirty-five years of marriage, he didn't know her at all.

ꙮ CHAPTER TWENTY-FOUR ꙮ

"Abbie knew that she was sick, but she tried to keep it from Billy. All he'd do is worry."
                                                    Charlotte Montgomery

Sunrise caught Abbie by surprise sitting cross-legged on the kitchen floor. Forks and spoons and plates and spatulas and the contents of a half dozen drawers lay around her in a tight semicircle. She recognized the signs. She had been looking for "it" again.

The blackouts were a recent development. She had lied to herself about what they meant. As she picked up the spilt flatware the truth dawned on her. She was going crazy, or more accurately, she had gone crazy. Billy had been right yesterday...she needed help. But so many regretful words had been thrown at each other across the cold, untouched dinner table.

Abbie felt the weight of yesterday's sleepless night settle onto her shoulders as she scooped up a handful of steak knives and spoons and took them to the sink. Through the kitchen door, she could see a masculine silhouette stretched out on the sofa. Billy hadn't woken up yet.

He was a handsome man. He appeared familiar but she couldn't be certain. She tiptoed into the living room to get a better look. Sure enough, the man on the couch resembled someone she had known years ago, a very nice person. She'd remember the name in a second, she was certain.

He opened his eyes and smiled. It was a very nice smile..

"Good morning, Abbie."

"You know my name," she said, a little surprised. "Have we met? Oh, that's silly, of course we have. You're sleeping on my couch, we *must* have met!" She gave a nervous laugh and then blushed with the realization that it was happening again.

"I *know* you," she said. She started to remember his name, but it wouldn't quite make it all the way to her tongue.

"You gonna use that, Abbie?" He was staring at her hand. She was still holding onto one of the steak knives.

She held it up and stared at the curving, sharp blade. Was she going to use it? No, she was going to... what? Why did she have the knife?

Her gaze shifted from the cold steel blade to the face on her couch. Why couldn't she remember who he was? He didn't seem to be a threat, but then why else was she holding a knife?

Abbie changed the way she gripped the weapon, pointing the blade backward and setting her thumb on the handle.

"Abbie, it's me," the man said. His eyes blinked rapidly and his voice was low and serious.

She was confused by the change in his face. Was it fear? Anger?

"Me who?" she demanded.

"Billy. I'm Billy." He held his left hand out in front of his chest and grabbed a couch pillow in his right. "Abigail, give me the knife," he told her. "Sweetie, it's me, Billy."

"Billy?" Her memory floodgate opened and she cried out, "*Billy*," dropping the knife onto the rug. Billy scooped it up and placed it on the phone table behind the couch.

There were more tears, but the fighting was over. Abbie packed a small overnight bag and walked to the car without looking back. She heard a small voice tell her she would return to Henderson Hill soon enough, but she didn't believe it.

෨ CHAPTER TWENTY-FIVE ෨

"It was for the best. It was for the best."
Charlotte Montgomery

Regency Nursing was a tidy apartment complex tucked away on the North side of Passable, a quick ten-minute drive from their home. The trip lasted hours. The walk from the parking lot into the "reception den" took days.

Abbie tagged along beside Billy, indifferent to the tour. She had no interest in meeting any of the staff. The charge nurse introduced herself, but Abbie didn't listen. The nurse was younger, with a superficial smile. Abbie despised her.

Four orderlies wandered about, picking up magazines and putting them into neat piles. Abbie watched them and wondered how old the magazines were. They looked old and grimy. One of the orderlies was a tall, thick black man called "Little Jim". He was very pleasant, at one point passing by Abbie and touching one finger to his forehead in a faux salute, saying "Ma'am". She found herself despising Little Jim a little bit less than she did the rest of the staff.

From the reception den, the charge nurse led Billy and Abbie on a walking tour through the Regency facilities. Billy took an interest in the exercise room, which, the nurse pointed out, had an attached indoor pool.

"Look at that, sweetheart. A swimming pool."

"I don't swim, William," she answered flatly. She used his formal name like a slap.

"Lunch time!" The booming voice belonged to Little Jim. He took over the tour from the charge nurse, and led the small group down an adjacent hallway.

Abbie was surprised by the dining room. She had already formed a mental image of an antiseptic, fiberglass and tile cafeteria. There would be three rows of tables, each with four plastic chairs and a napkin dispenser. The room would smell like Clorox and meat loaf.

Instead, the dining room was cozy and warm. Reading chairs dotted its perimeter, tucked in between bookcases and green library lamps. In the center of the polished wood floor sat two large walnut tables, each surrounded by more than a dozen chairs. They dominated the room without being overpowering.

Perhaps it was hunger, but Abbie found she didn't despise the dining room. She sat with Billy and Little Jim at a side table and enjoyed a light lunch of string beans with onions and bacon bits, sweet tea, and crab salad.

Slowly at first, then swelling into a flood, she overflowed with questions. Can Billy stay here with me? Do I have a phone? Can I leave and go home?

No, Billy would not be allowed to stay. No visitors were allowed in the dormitory area.

No, residents did not have phones in their rooms.

No, residents were not normally allowed to leave the Regency for extended periods of time. Abigail would not be permitted to leave for at least a month. The court order had imposed the restriction.

Abbie was stunned at the mention of a court order. Billy hadn't said anything about that. She thought moving into the nursing home was voluntary, maybe even temporary.

A court order! This was no visit – it was a trap.

Her appetite gone, she folded her napkin and tossed it onto her plate, then stood and asked Little Jim to take her to her quarters. Immediately. She glared at Billy, accusing him with her eyes.

"Yes, ma'am," Little Jim said. "Right this way." He guided her out of the dining hall into the den, and then to a tan colored steel fireproof door with an engraved plastic sign that said 'DORMITORY'.

Billy hurried along behind them, weakly calling her name, begging her to slow down, to wait for him.

Little Jim pushed the handle and the steel door opened into a hotel-like hallway. "You're in room 103. Second door on the left," he pointed to her room and she went straight in.

Billy followed about five yards back. "Abbie," he called out, "wait, wait a moment…"

Little Jim blocked Billy from reaching Abbie. "I'm sorry sir, residents only in the dorm area. You'll have to leave."

"In a minute," Billy objected. "Abbie, wait…"

"Sir…" Little Jim started.

Abbie interrupted, "Wait for what? You have another *surprise* for me?"

"You can't go like this!" Billy insisted.

"Like what? I'm not going anywhere. *I'm not allowed to.*"

Little Jim placed his hand on Billy's chest and repeated the house rules, "Sir, you'll have to leave now…"

"Yes," Abbie chimed in, "You have to leave now."

"This isn't right," Billy cried. "I never…I only…"

"Sir. Leave *now.*"

Billy looked up into Little Jim's eyes. The black man was taller than him by six full inches and outweighed him by fifty pounds. "Get out of my way." Billy's tone of voice carried the calm deliberation of a rattlesnake. He watched Abbie disappear through the door to room 103, closing it behind her. His heart and his patience broke.

Little Jim shifted his hand slightly. He moved it from the center of Billy's chest and placed it squarely on his left shoulder. "Let me show you out," he said, turning Billy counter-clockwise. It was the opening the smaller man needed. His old Army training took over.

Looping his right arm over Little Jim's left, he twisted on his heels and locked Little Jim in a painful elbow trap. Then Billy balled up his left hand and aimed a hammer blow directly at the big man's temple.

Three decades earlier, the maneuver would have dropped an enemy soldier to his knees. But Billy hadn't practiced hand-to-hand combat since boot camp.

"Damn! Ow!" he whimpered, cradling his hand and checking it for broken bones.

"Ow! Why'd ya hit me, man?" Little Jim asked, covering his nose with his free hand. "Get outa here 'fore I gets mad!" He shoved Billy backwards through the open dormitory door.

Billy tucked his head low and plowed into the big man's midsection, folding him in half and driving both men back into the dormitory. They rolled to the side and slammed into the wall before falling to the floor in a clinch. With his good hand, Billy punched like a boxer at Little Jim's kidneys.

"Ow! Stop hittin' me," Little Jim grunted. Billy pulled himself free and backed away, leaving Little Jim laid out in the middle of the hall.

The door to room 103 opened and Abbie stuck her head out into the hallway. "Billy!" she scolded. "What are you *doing*?"

Billy half-turned with both fists held low, bouncing lightly on the balls of his feet, standing over the fallen form of the large black orderly. He looked into her eyes and saw a young bride standing there, barely eighteen. "Abbie," he said, "I..."

Little Jim had long legs and Billy didn't see the kick coming. His foot hit Bill from below, punching all the air out of his lungs and driving him backward through the dormitory door and into the reception area. His head hit the floor hard.

Billy smelled blood and woke up confused. A doctor's penlight was flashing on and off, making his eyes hurt. He tried to sit up, but a firm hand pushed him back down against the floor.

"Billy? Can you hear me?" It was the voice of Ben James, the town constable. "You just stay down there and relax, y'hear?"

It sounded like good advice. Billy's hand hurt, his ribs hurt, and his head hurt. "How's the other guy?" Billy asked weakly.

Little Jim looked down on him from far above. "I'm okay, mistuh Dare," he said. "Sorry 'bout kickin' you."

Billy nodded in his direction. "That's all right. Barely felt it."

The constable peered at Billy's face, checking to make sure the older man would be sufficiently conscious to follow orders. "Mister Dare, I'm constable Ben James."

"I know who you are."

"Sir, I'm placing you under arrest. You're going to have to come with me and I won't tolerate any nonsense. Are you going to behave yourself or do we need the handcuffs?"

"I'm all fighted out," Billy said. Ben James helped him to his feet, keeping a firm grasp above his elbow. Together, they walked out to the patrol car. The constable helped Billy get into the back seat, which was separated from the driver's seat by a thick wire screen.

The blue police lights were turned off as the two men drove away from the Regency. Billy was lucid enough to recognize the street they were on. They were going the wrong way.

"Ben, the jail's in the other direction."

"Did you hear me read you your rights?"

"Now that you mention it, no."

"I'm taking you home."

"Great," he answered flatly.

"I'm sorry to hear about Abbie," he offered.

"Yeah."

"You had to do it, Billy. She could get hurt."

"Yeah, thanks."

They drove up Henderson Hill and parked in front of the house. Constable James opened the rear door so Billy could get out.

"Don't get into any more fistfights, okay?" he warned.

"Sure."

"I mean it, Bill." He got back into the squad car and rolled down the window. "I'll pick you up at seven AM sharp." He started the engine and put the car in reverse.

"What for?" Billy asked.

"You'll need a ride back to the Regency to get your car," Ben explained.

"Oh. I forgot."

"And you ought to be there when Abbie wakes up. I hear tell that they serve up a real good breakfast at that place," he said.

Billy thanked the constable. He only used the two most essential words, but it was obvious he really meant it. The squad car pulled out into the road and a few seconds later was gone.

Billy walked up the steps and unlocked the front door. He stood in the hallway for a few long seconds, listening to the coarse tink-tink-tink of the wall clock. It was the only sound in the house.

❧ CHAPTER TWENTY-SIX ❧

"Abbie brought her problems to the Regency. Billy hoped they
could help. I suppose they tried their best."
                                    Charlotte Montgomery

The first light of morning snuck in through a break in the
curtains. It formed a bright line that slid slowly down the wall
as the sun tracked higher in the early dawn sky. Abbie winced
awake a few minutes later, her eyes assaulted by the brightness.

Squinting, she reached over to see whether Bill was
awake. They had a busy day planned. He was taking her to
Belk's to buy a new dress for dinner with Dr. Brighton.

Her hand found the edge of the bed where a pillow should
have been. An alarm went off in her mind...*not my bed.* Her
eyes snapped open.

"Billy?" She probed the little room with her voice. Billy
wasn't there. Abbie didn't recognize the bed. She looked
around at the dizzying strangeness of the room and swallowed
the panic welling up inside her.

"Billy?"

The memories of the night before crept back, slowly
building a puzzle with pieces missing. She searched for
slippers and found a pair beneath the bed, but they weren't
hers. She briefly debated wearing them anyway, but decided

they looked too large. She had a thousand questions that couldn't wait for perfect slippers, so bare feet would just have to do.

She pulled her robe tighter around her throat and padded into the hallway. She heard voices outside the dormitory door. There would be answers in that direction.

Abbie pulled the hallway door open and stuck her head through. Three younger women dressed in lime green scrubs were gathered around a coffee pot, sharing private gossip. The one who was speaking, a black girl with close-cropped hair, saw Abbie peek into the common area.

"Good morning, Abbie," she said. "Are we finished getting dressed, dear?"

Abigail was put off by the familiarity of the greeting. "Mrs. Dare" would have been more appropriate. But people were strange, so she let the moment pass without comment.

"Where…" she stopped, shocked by the hoarseness in her own voice. She cleared her throat and tried a second time, "Where is Billy?"

She had treated Billy so shabbily last night. He didn't deserve to get hauled off by the constable. He was only trying to find a way to say "good night" and then the fight started. She had been so proud that he would take on someone the size of Little Jim. Billy was her rock. She needed to apologize.

"Is my Billy here, yet?"

"No, ma'am," the nurse said, "he hasn't called today. Maybe a little later." She left her gossip circle and joined Abbie in the hallway. "You want breakfast, Abbie? You know you can't walk around without somethin' on your feet. C'mon, let's find you some clothes." She guided Abigail back to her room.

"Who are you?" Abbie asked. "What's your name?"

"I'm Candy," the nurse answered. "Don't you remember? Candy? Sweetest nurse at Regency?" She flashed her winningest smile at Abbie.

"No, I'm sorry. I must not have been paying attention when we met." She couldn't remember this nurse at all. When she checked in, she remembered seeing two, or was it three, nurses, but not this one.

"That's all right," Candy said, guiding Abbie into her room.

Abbie shuddered to a stop and stared at the floor where Billy and Little Jim had fought the night before. She hadn't seen the end of the fight, but remembered how hard Billy had hit the larger man.

"Little Jim – is he all right? I do hope that he wasn't seriously hurt."

"Who?" Candy asked.

"Little Jim. The big orderly Billy fought with last night. Is he okay?"

"Oh, you must mean Jim Carver," Candy answered, shaking her head. "Never met him, but I'd heard he was a big man."

"Never met him?"

"No, ma'am. He was gone before I got here."

"I thought he was on the day shift," Abbie commented.

"No, ma'am. I'm sorry. I meant *gone*. Cancer took him last year. I thought you knew, Miss Abbie. I thought you knew 'bout mister Carver's passing."

"How could I know that?" she shot back. "That's *stupid*, that's all. I met Little Jim just yesterday. He helped me move in…"

Candy shook her head, "No Miss Abbie…"

"…Jim and Billy got into an awful fight…"

Candy's instincts kicked in. She was on the edge of a confrontation and the patient care rules were strict about arguments. "Oh, that's right, Miss Abbie, I remember now, I was all mixed up there for a second…"

"Billy should be here by now," Abbie said, aloof. "He's always here for breakfast, you know. He's almost never late." Nurse Candy guided her back to the room and helped her find something suitable to wear.

Candy finished laying out some day clothes while Abbie washed her face and neck with a hot washcloth. Then she excused herself and returned to the nurse's station.

Two nurses were already there, scribbling notes in the records when Candy came into the work area. "Anybody know how long Abbie Dare has been a resident here?" she asked.

The older of the two nurses remembered. The name MILLER was on her nametag. "I think she checked in back around '76," she said with a sharp drawl. "So she's been here eight years, give or take."

"It's astounding that she still talks about Billy," Candy opined.

The youngest nurse offered her opinion. "I thought he was one of her imaginary people," she said.

"No, Billy was real. He was her husband. Except for the first day, he was a wonderful old gent. He never missed breakfast with Abbie, not in five long years."

"You said *eight* years," the youngest nurse pointed out. "Abbie has been here for eight years, not five."

"Oh, her husband passed on in '81 or '82," Miller answered.

Candy asked, "How did he die?"

"Cain't say," Miller commented, "but I'm thinking that puttin' his wife in here killed him. I watched him turn old and gray right in front of my eyes."

"Pneumonia, I heard," the young nurse said.

"Who knows?" Miller answered. "We heard he had died nearly a week after the fact. Might've been the pneumonia, but I think he was just plum wore out." She signed the patient record she was working on and took a deep breath, searching her memory. "The last time I saw mister Billy, it was winter. December, I think, but I don't remember the exact date. He showed up at breakfast lookin' just *awful*. I overheard him saying that he'd been workin' the garden in the rain the night before and now was all stove up. Then Abbie got mad at him for plantin' winter crops so late in the spring. Her mind was in pretty bad shape by then."

"So now she relives that same day over and over," Candy added, shaking her head. "I guess she couldn't accept his death."

"What? Oh, no," Miller corrected her. "Abbie doesn't know mister Billy is dead. We never told her."

Candy was shocked. "Are you serious? That's cruel. Not to mention malpractice."

"It's only cruel if we tell her about it now," the young nurse said.

Candy couldn't believe what she was hearing. "But the doctor is supposed to notify patients when there's a death in the family. It's Regency policy."

"That was the problem," Miller explained, "The day before mister Billy died, our doctor took a job with Anderson Hospital and the Regency couldn't find a replacement for two weeks. Then the new one up and quit without telling Abbie about Bill, and the next three doctors didn't last through Christmas. Next thing you know, it's a year later and nobody's told Abbie that she's a widow."

"This is unacceptable. We can't keep hiding this from her," Candy complained. She made a mental note to discuss this problem with Dr. Hennessee, their fresh new board certified geriatric specialist.

"Where is Abbie?" Candy asked. "She was supposed to be coming out for breakfast." She looked around the common area but didn't see Abbie anywhere. "I'd better look in on her," she said. She had been away from Room 103 for almost ten minutes.

Abbie was sitting on the floor naked, her legs crossed and her neatly folded clothes balled up on either side of her. The sheets, blankets and pillows had been pulled off the bed and piled in the corner. Every drawer had been emptied and the drawers themselves tossed aside. The bathroom cabinet had been swept into the sink, except for a small bottle of aspirin, which had fallen into the toilet.

Weeping quietly to herself, Abbie was emptying her purse onto the floor, examining each key, lipstick, and tissue she pulled out. "No, no, no…" she repeated as she tossed them aside.

"Oh, Abbie!" Candy said, exasperated. "Not again."

"I can't find it," Abigail repeated. "I can't find it."

ᕲ CHAPTER TWENTY-SEVEN ᕰ

*"God in his mercy limits how much pain we have to endure.
Sometimes he touches us and takes the agony away.
Sometimes he uses angels."*
Charlotte Montgomery

In '84, winter's first frost blew in early. Halloween was too cold for trick-or-treats, but just right for freezing rain. The Regency hadn't had a chance to finish maintenance on their heating system, so most of the residents pulled their winter sweaters out of storage and wore them to breakfast.

Abbie padded out into the common area in her bare feet. The floor was cold but she was looking for her constant breakfast companion and didn't care whether her feet hurt.

He was late, again. No doubt her father had engaged Billy in some silly political discussion. That, or maybe he just forgot. Abbie would tell the other residents that William Dare would forget his own name if she didn't get mad and yell it at him from time to time.

The nursing staff huddled around the television, listening to the weather report. *"Unusual ice storm across the southeast,"* the lady on the screen was telling the camera. *"Early winter..."*

Abbie worked her way closer to the dining room. The floor was icy cold on her arches, but Billy should never be left waiting.

"...*fewer horseflies next summer...*"

Nurse Candy spotted Abbie shuffling along without any shoes. The look on her face warned Abbie a scolding was coming her way.

"Damn!" she cursed quietly. That little black woman could be so unbearable. Abbie did a quick about-face and shuffled across the new, cold tile floor back to her room. She hated that tile. There was nothing wrong with the old carpet.

"Miss Abbie? Did you throw a shoe?" Nurse Candy called after her. "Put on some decent clothes and come on out for some pancakes."

"Is Billy here yet?" Abbie yelled back from her room.

"No, ma'am, he's not," she answered. "Don't let me catch you unshod in the dining room, y'hear?"

"I like the other nurse better," Abbie grunted.

This cold weather would play havoc on her garden. If only she were outside, at her house, she could tend to whatever the garden needed. "*I have the knack for it,*" she whispered to herself. "*I have the knack.*"

She liked the way the little phrase sounded, starting off all soft and breathless and ending with a guttural click. She told herself she would have to remember to use "I have the knack" in a sentence sometime today. Billy would be here soon, and surely he'd have to agree that when it came to gardening, she had the knack.

Abbie sat in the dining room, politely deflecting requests for company. She explained to each requestor that Billy was late, but would surely be here soon and the chair next to her was reserved for him. This usually meant she would sit alone and eat nothing, waiting for someone who would never arrive.

Abigail's innocent dementia infuriated Myra Luckworth, a relatively new arrival who was restricted to moving about in a wheelchair. Her temper-red hair was never brushed and gave her the look of a mad revolutionary, or maybe a Bohemian poet. Myra's unconstrained behavior in public added to her unsavory reputation.

She pulled out Bill's chair and rolled her own into the open space. "Hey! Garcon!" she shouted. "We're starving out here!"

From the kitchen came the familiar voice of the Regency's chef, answering the call of the wild redhead. "Good!" she said, "You'll die soon and I won't have to cook for y'all no more!"

"Hellooo, Abbie!" Myra beamed a big smile in her direction.

"B-Bill is coming soon," she told Myra. She would have insisted his chair be returned to its proper place at the table, but was unable to be even remotely rude to a person in a wheelchair. "He'll be here any minute."

"Probably not," Myra dismissed her, turning her attention to the plates of pancakes being delivered by the cook.

"One stack of buttermilk cakes for you, sweetie," the cook told Abbie, setting the plate softly on the table. Then she scowled at Myra and dropped the second plate in front of her from a full inch above the wood. The bacon, soggy and undercooked, jumped off the plate and soiled the napkin. "Bone appateet."

"Bitch," Myra said.

Abbie fidgeted with her fork, unsure whether to cut into the meal before Billy arrived. It would be so rude.

"Quit pickin' and eat! D'ya like maple syrup?" Before Abbie could politely explain that she preferred her pancakes with butter only, Myra poured half a cup of the sweet-smelling liquid onto Abbie's pancakes. "Eat 'em up. We gotta go buy you a black dress today."

This was so much fun! She hadn't been at the Regency for a whole month and yet she already knew about The Big Billy Lie. She figured this morning would be a perfect time to fill in the blanks in this stupid old woman's life.

"I don't need a black dress," Abbie commented. "Why would I want one?"

"Bill ain't comin'," she said, drenching her own pancakes in maple syrup and shoving a forkful into her mouth.

"Oh, of course he is."

"Not today!" Myra chirped happily.

"What do you mean?" Abbie asked. "Have you heard something?"

"Oh, boy, *have* I!"

Nurse Miller ran in behind Myra Luckworth and wrenched her wheelchair away from the table. "Scuse us, Abbie. Myra and I need to have a little girl talk."

"What? Where are we...?" Myra objected. She reached for the brakes but the nurse was quick and saw the move.

"Touch those brakes and I'll hack off yer fingers," Miller hissed.

"Where are we going?" Myra balled up her fists to protect her fingers.

"We? *We* ain't goin' nowhere, not right now, not *us*," she said, laughing at her own joke.

As Miller pushed the wheelchair past the nurse's station, Myra turned and blurted out weakly, "Help me!"

Nurse Candy smiled and waved.

Nurse Miller pushed the wheelchair out the front door, turned right, and headed to the edge of the parking lot. She stopped and locked the brakes at the top of a steep embankment. The short, frostbitten lawn bent downward like a ski slope. At the bottom, thirty feet down, was a live creek guarded on all sides by thick kudzu vines.

"Take a real good look, Myra," the nurse said. "Imagine yerself riding this here wheelchair down into that bog. I wonder how cold that water must be. Oh, dear, yer shivering. D'ya wanna go back inside?"

"Y-yes! Let's go back!"

Miller casually pulled out a cigarette and lit it. Myra didn't smoke, wouldn't smoke, and couldn't tolerate even a hint of burning tobacco. She fanned her hand in front of her face and wrinkled her nose, but the nurse ignored the hint.

When the cigarette was half gone, she stubbed it out with her foot and walked back toward the Regency, alone.

After a few steps, she called out, "Don't be too long out here. Yer not dressed for this weather."

Myra wanted to run the old nurse down but all she had was her wheelchair, still perched dizzyingly close to the drop-off over the bog. She released the brakes and cautiously pulled the wheels back away from the edge, toward the cold safety of the parking lot. She pulled the wheels back, but they were stuck on something and refused her efforts to move.

"Need a little help?"

Myra hadn't heard nurse Miller come back. The way she was standing behind the wheelchair, she couldn't see her at all.

"Get away from me," Myra demanded, pulling harder on the wheels. This time they spun in place but the chair still didn't move.

"You need to be nicer to people," the old voice said.

"Screw you."

"Listen to me, Myra Luckworth, and pay close attention." Hidden by shadows, her voice sounded far away, a distant breeze of words worrying the tree branches just before a storm. "You may be an evil bitch, but that's no excuse for being stupid, too. You are all alone in this world. You have nobody. No children. No husband. No kin. You are exactly like Abigail Dare, except for one little difference. Everybody loves Abbie."

"You won't get away with this," Myra tried to say, but the shivering was making it hard to talk. She struggled to make the wheels take her back to the asphalt.

"Need a little help?" the nurse repeated cruelly, thunder in her meaning. Myra pulled harder on the wheels but the chair shuddered and slipped slightly sideways, skidding closer to the embankment. The nurse! The damned nurse was pushing the chair forward!

The front wheels stopped inches from the downturn of the grassy slope. The old nurse's tone never changed, soft and factual. "I'll bet that if you fell into that bog and everybody heard you screaming in your final agonizing seconds of life, they would all take their time finding their overcoats before coming outside. They would *walk* over here and look."

The voice shifted slightly, coming from over Myra's left shoulder.

"Nobody would run."

Then it shifted again, this time from Myra's right.

"Nobody would miss you."

Then from behind the wheelchair.

"Nobody would mourn you."

Then distantly, from everywhere, slowly and with the softness of a mother cooing to her child.

"Nobody… loves… you."

Myra wrenched the wheels backward again. This time her chair answered with a brisk roll and thump as it hit the hard surface of the parking lot. She glimpsed the nurse walking in the shadows toward the Regency and gasped when she saw the old woman's feet.

They were absolutely bare – no socks, no shoes, no sandals – and in this weather. Laughing bitterly, she yelled, "Hey! What were you *thinking*? What's *wrong* with you?"

'…wrong with you…' Myra's voice echoed off the Regency. The yellow blaze of the streetlights cast strange shadows that swallowed the barefoot nurse in darkness, trapping her ankles and toes in a soft glow.

"It's all right, Miss Luckworth," the shadows said, "I don't have very far to go." She stepped out of the light and was gone before Myra could wheel herself back inside the unfriendly warmth of the Regency.

Nurse Miller sat with Abbie. "That hateful woman," Miller told her. "Can you believe it? She said she wasn't hungry."

Abbie reached out and held Miller's arm. "She said something about Billy. That he wasn't coming, or something"

"Oh, it's this dang freeze," the old nurse said with a happy smile. "I'll bet mister Billy is frost-proofing the garden."

Abbie considered this, looked serious and said, "Oh, probably so. But I do wish he'd talk to me first. He's not very good at that sort of thing."

"I've heard tell *you're* a whiz at gard'nin'," Miller added.

Abbie grinned. "I have the knack!"

Nurse Miller moved Bill's reserved seat back into its place, patted Abbie on the shoulder, and walked back to the nurses' station, passing Myra Luckworth on the way. The two ladies didn't speak. In the station, Candy said "Miz Luckworth just came by, all agitated and sayin' that you tried to kill her, and making a fuss about your feet. What do you suppose she meant by all that?"

"Beats me. I was in the dining hall with Abbie."

"I'll speak to the doctor about boosting Myra's Elavil."

In the dining room, Abigail had slowly eaten two tiny bites of soggy pancakes, a nibble of bacon, and a small glass of V-8 juice. She folded and unfolded her napkin sixteen times, finally balling it up and laying it in the center of the table.

She stared at her plate as though it were a television. Abbie could see images of Billy and Henderson Hill, pictures of her garden burnt by the early frost. And Billy was wearing his old denim jacket. Why, that old rag had holes in it and would never protect him from the cutting cold air. She grumbled, "He ought to wait for me."

The staff at Regency never knew what it was that triggered Abbie's compulsive searching, but the signs were all there – the frown, the fidgeting, the nervous wandering. This morning, she was thumbing through all the magazines in the reception area. "Southern Farm Home" seemed to be her favorite. She actually read part of a page in an old summer issue. Other reading material barely registered.

Pretty soon, they'd have to intervene. If they timed it just right, they could slip her a little Valium and avoid a major cleanup. Nurse Candy wanted to give her the shot right now, but the house physician had firm rules about the use of drugs for behavioral restraint.

Lunchtime came and went without any trouble. Nurse Candy approached Abigail with the suggestion she might want to change out of her dressing gown and put on something a little more appropriate. Abbie answered she had some jeans somewhere and excused herself to go look.

In a sudden shot of panic, Candy realized she might have just triggered a Search. She reached out and gripped Abbie's arm, tugging her gently toward the dining room. "That's really not necessary, Miss Abbie," she said as calmly as she could. "If y'all are comfy in that nightgown and robe, then they'll do for lunch."

"Oh, but I'm sure I have some pants in the closet…"

"…No, ma'am, don't you trouble yourself…"

"…and more comfortable shoes…"

"…you're dressed just *perfect*." Winning the argument at last, Nurse Candy guided Abbie through the dining room door.

"These sandals pinch," Abbie complained. From across the room, a woman with a messy red hairdo grabbed half a sandwich and hurriedly wheeled her chair out the door. "Hello," Abbie called out, waving. For a fleeting second, the woman looked familiar.

Without knowing exactly why, Abbie started worrying about Bill again. She sat for lunch but didn't eat. Her thoughts raced. Billy shouldn't be out in weather like this. Not in such a shabby old jacket. And he really had no knack for gardening.

Abbie processed and re-processed this train of thought over and over. Two hours passed, but she didn't notice. She forgot she was in the lunchroom. For a second she almost remembered something she had read in "Southern Farm Home," something important. Something she couldn't quite put her finger on.

She got up and walked around the dining room. The reading chairs were gone. They had been there just a moment earlier, but now they were gone! It was so frustrating the way people kept changing things without any good reason and without telling anybody.

"No matter," she told herself. What she really needed was that copy of "Southern Farm Home". It had a fine article on something that was probably important. She couldn't remember what it was about, exactly, but it would help Billy in the garden. Abbie wandered around the empty dining room, checking each table without finding a single magazine.

She walked into a short hallway she supposed might lead her back to her room. The magazine was probably in the dormitory, she was sure of it. It wouldn't be difficult to find. But this hallway was different than the one she remembered. There were only two doors in it. One of them led into the kitchen. Abbie looked through that door, but there was nobody on the other side.

The second door was made of metal, painted dull brown. It was cracked open about a foot and the bright afternoon sun blazed through from the other side. Abbie pushed her head through the opening and squinted. Her breath steamed away in the crisp breeze. She had never been on this side of the Regency. The heavy metal door opened easily. Rounding the corner, she heard it slam shut.

❧ CHAPTER TWENTY-EIGHT ❧

"The need to go home is as unyielding as steel, more important to the human spirit than flesh and bone, more powerful than life itself."

Charlotte Montgomery

Abbie walked back to the fire door and tested the handle. It was locked tight. This worried her a little, but then she remembered she could always get back inside through the front entrance. She laughed to herself thinking about how silly the nurses would look, seeing her traipse back inside unannounced.

But she hadn't been outside by herself in ages and it didn't feel that cold, with the afternoon sun warming up the parking lot. Abbie explored farther from the Regency's walls, away from the comforting brick and over to the outer edge of the asphalt. She stood on top of an embankment looking down on a bog surrounded in tangle foot. And something else caught her eye. Something on the other side of the swamp. A glint of steel.

Railroad tracks! A thin pair of steel ribbons peeked out above the kudzu and disappeared back into the woods. They reminded her of the tracks that crossed Henderson Road, only a mile or two south of her home.

As she stared at the tracks, Abbie became convinced that she could follow them and they could lead her home. Home, to Billy, who must surely be freezing cold by now. She'd have to make him some soup, and a pot of hot coffee. Home, to the garden.

She wasted no time deciding what to do. Abbie stepped over the curb and onto the frost-slick slope. Her feet shot out from under her, plopping her onto her backside and knocking the wind from her lungs. In a flash, she was out of sight and sliding helplessly toward the dark water below.

Her feet sticking straight up in the air, Abbie skipped across the vegetation on the near side of the bog and splashed to a stop neatly in the middle of the swamp. The water was thigh-deep and not quite frozen, with a flat mud bottom. Her ankles and knees screamed with pain from the icy cold but she ignored them and slogged across, pulling herself up and over the opposite bank using the kudzu vines as rope.

Her slippers remained behind, firmly glued to the bog's muddy floor. Abbie didn't care. Her heart had made up its mind. She was going home!

The railroad tracks sat atop a raised embankment draped in gravel. From a distance, the white stones looked smooth and inviting, but their jagged edges pricked at Abbie's feet, etching tiny slices across the bottoms of her toes and heels. The cold water had numbed her from the knees down, so she didn't notice the cuts and she didn't look back. If she had, the bloodstained rocks might have convinced her to return to the Regency.

Abbie followed the tracks, stepping carefully from crosstie to crosstie. A mile of walking, stumbling and shivering inside a bog-soaked nightgown left her too tired to be careful. She tripped on a loose tie and sprawled onto the gravel between the rails. "*Old fool!*" she chided herself, wiping a bloody palm on her nightgown. Her knees ached from the effort of getting back up. Home *couldn't* be far away. Abbie pushed herself harder.

The tracks bored through the pines, a green and brown tunnel guiding Abigail around a gentle curve and spilling out of the woods onto a wide, gray field. On the left, a cement plant stood at the head of a rail yard. Hopper cars lined up beneath its silo, waiting to be filled with the heavy powder. Dust blossoming out of their filler hatches had settled around the yard, coating everything in a layer of gray silt.

Each step she took kicked up a dust cloud, clinging heavily to her nightgown, crusting around her mouth and gripping her with an impossible thirst. She forced her feet to march on – left foot, right foot, left foot – past the silos and back into the woods, following the tracks.

The tiny cuts on her soles forced Abbie to slow down and step delicately, but the afternoon shadows draped the treetops, adding urgency to her pace. She shuffled along, leaving behind a trail of caked cement and flecks of red on the sugar-white gravel.

Two hours of mincing down the tracks on torn feet yielded barely more than a mile of progress. Her feet wanted to stop and rest but daylight would be ending soon - too soon. Abbie couldn't ignore the pain and she couldn't make it go away, so she decided to do the next best thing and just let it hurt.

She swallowed hard and forced her feet to move faster, taking longer strides and putting ground behind her. Exhausted, she was walking on the legs of a stranger, moving on their own as she looked down and watched them from above.

Had Abigail looked up half a second later, she might have walked straight into the towering diesel engine blocking her path. Large as it was, it was hard to see, the yellows and reds of the welded steel plates drained of their original brilliance by years of kerosene smoke and the dwindling light of the day.

She touched it delicately. *"How did you sneak up on me?"* she asked. Searching for a way around, she crossed the rail on the left hand side and found an uneven path. Halfway down the length of the engine, a bushy thicket of briars and scrub oak sprouting out of the woods blocked her way.

Abbie backtracked around the engine and crossed to the foot trail on the other side. There were wild plants growing there, too, but she forced her way past them and finally made it to the back of the locomotive. Behind it was another behemoth, a rusted, empty boxcar. And then another, and two more…a long chain of boxcars, flatbeds, and hoppers filled with more gray cement, stretching into the distance.

She worked her way down the line of cars. The footing was narrow and uneven, making progress slow. Halfway past the fourth car, she was once again blocked by a copse of wild briars. There was only one way to get to the other side of the train, but the thought of crawling under the railroad cars terrified her. When she was little, Hyram told her horror stories about children being squashed while playing near trains. But daylight was vanishing steadily and she was more afraid of the dark than she was of being crushed.

Abbie laid her body flat against the nearest rail, held her breath and rolled under the train. The ground beneath the boxcar smelled of urine… and worse. It took years to get to the other side. She emerged filthy and cold, reeking of whatever putrescence had soaked into the ground between the rails.

Darkness forced her to hurry, to make her feet move faster. Three more times, wild patches of prickly underbrush stopped her, and three more times, she edged her way under the cars to the other side.

The sky turned dark purple. Abbie had to keep one hand on the train for balance and walk slower, and slower still, until finally she couldn't see enough to walk at all. The train and the tracks and the path and the briars were invisible in the cold black of night.

The wind whipped the tops of the pines, sending icy eddies swirling down the footpath and forcing Abbie under the nearest boxcar, huddled in a ball and shivering uncontrollably. Soon, the full moon rose high enough to paint the ground with soft shadows, lighting the path for Abbie to see where she was going again.

Shortly before midnight, she picked her way past the final car on the train. Her feet moved faster beneath her, carrying her weight more easily, taking her closer to home with every step, and then they skipped a step and stumbled to a stop, her arms flailing for balance.

The ground had turned flat and hard and smooth. Abbie knelt to feel it with her hand. The gravel was gone and the ground was strangely warm ... asphalt! The tracks crossed over a road, but which road?

She looked around but saw no signs. In the moon's light, the road appeared to travel uphill. It might have been her imagination or an illusion of shadows, but the slope of the road looked right, somehow. Abbie trusted her instincts. This had to be Henderson Road. She started walking up the hill.

The moon rose higher, brighter, and showed Abigail more details. But it had been so many years. The angle and twist of the road seemed right, but the landmarks were all wrong – a dirt road where an ancient oak should have been, a mobile home where she remembered a pine thicket. And then she saw it... a guardrail, bending sharply to the left. Even by moonlight, Abbie recognized Dead Man's Curve. Only half a mile to home! Her heart leapt at the thought.

The wind picked up speed, pouring out of the north with face-cutting ferocity. Thinking only of Billy and home, she quickened her pace and pushed against the wind. The wind pushed back, opening her robe and stealing what little warmth it had to offer.

Filled with energy meant for the young, Abbie broke into a jog, stumbling and tearing the skin from her left knee. Furious at her own clumsiness, she settled into a fast march instead. The wind bit and tugged, and the road tore at her feet, but Abbie just pushed herself harder, marching faster up Henderson Road, and then...

She didn't believe it. Her eyes were looking directly at it, and still she didn't believe it. The windows were broken and the brick was crumbling in the corners. Vines were scaling the walls, threatening to pull the old house to the ground, back down into the abandoned cow pasture Billy had bought after the war.

Abbie had found her way home.

Forgetting the pain in her feet, she sprinted like a teenager around the side of her beautiful, freshly painted house and stopped at the edge of the wild and overgrown corner that used to be her garden. It glowed under the moonlight, revealing everything. Beans and corn and collards, all in perfect rows and ready for picking. The tomatoes and peppers, heavy on the vines and ripe and beautiful! Even the garlic was growing better than she could remember.

Humming to herself, Abigail returned to the front door and twisted the knob. The door swung into the hallway without any resistance and she walked into her own home for the first time in more than eight years. Just inside, a pair of glass-paned double French doors opened wide, welcoming her.

There were no chairs, but she was content to sit and rest on the hallway floor, where she had kissed Billy the night they tore down the wall. The pain in her feet eased and her legs stopped burning. Abbie no longer needed to fight for every breath. She was warm and safe, and she was home.

Knowing that Billy would be along soon, she propped her head against one of the doors and slept. Winter's cruelty lifted, leaving behind a blanket of white frost and a gentle summer breeze.

✣ CHAPTER TWENTY-NINE ✣

"Ben James hadn't been up to the old Dare place in nearly a year, ever since the county ordered him to padlock all the doors."

Charlotte Montgomery

Something had been bothering Constable James since two o'clock and he couldn't get back to sleep. He wasn't sure exactly what it was that had robbed him of half a night's rest – maybe it was a bad dream. Ben didn't remember having a nightmare, but then again he almost never remembered his dreams. He was a practical man, a responsible man.

It was 4:15 in the morning but Ben was alert and enjoying the icy moonlight drive down Henderson Road. Such a bright moon was a rare event, made even more intense by the clear night sky. The frost that had formed on top of the ground glowed white as snow, giving Henderson Hill a surreal and dizzying appearance.

The north edge of the old Dare place passed by on the left and the abandoned house soon appeared in his windshield, brightly lit from above. Ben glanced at it as he rolled past, barely registering the brief glimpse of a strange black shadow on the front porch.

"That's not right," he said to himself.

He turned around and came back to the driveway, flicking on his light bar. He flashed his searchlight on the front of the house and panned the full length. The garage was empty, no surprise there. The brick was cracked in places and ivy vines were reaching up into the windows. He pointed the beam further left and – there – a tall rectangular shadow, out of place only if you were looking for it. The front door was open, and wouldn't you know it, the padlock was gone!

"Damn kids," he muttered. Teenagers were always doing stupid stuff like this – breaking into abandoned houses for fun. He set the parking brake and got out with his flashlight in one hand.

He swept the faint circle of light left and right, then stopped and held steady on a set of small footprints etched deep into the icy layer of frost. They formed a trail that looked easy enough to follow in moonlight, but Ben used his flashlight anyway. The tracks took him around the side and into the old back yard where Abbie used to have a garden. Whoever had come back here hadn't gone any farther.

The footprints overlapped and the trail became muddled and indistinct. Ben shone his light in a wide circle and found a line of crisp tracks close to the house, hidden in the moon's shadow. They were evenly spaced and led directly to the front porch. Whoever the intruder was, they knew exactly where they were going.

Constable James followed the line of prints up the front steps and paused to look around for the missing padlock. There was no sign of it. Somebody had come out here just to steal that lock. *"No, that doesn't make any sense,"* he thought.

The front door was slightly ajar, so Ben pushed it open the rest of the way and lit up the hall with his flashlight. "Oh, Abbie," he sighed, bending down to test her pulse. Her skin was as cold as the ground and the stiffness of recent death froze Abigail Dare in place, leaning against one of the glass-paned doors.

⁂

"She was smiling," Charlotte Montgomery said. "Imagine that. Smiling. Well, the coroner came and took her away and you'd think that would be the end of it, wouldn't you? I mean, they laid that poor woman in the ground two days later and that should have ended the story, don't you think?"

"But remember, the constable stopped because the front door was open and the padlock was missing. It was nowhere around. Now, this is important because it wasn't a cheap padlock. It was one of the real pricey kind house sellers use. The county supervisor had paid for it with county funds and Constable James had signed it out. If he didn't find it, they'd dock his pay."

"It was all dark and cold in that house. When the coroner came, he brought an ambulance with him and those boys had portable battery-powered fluorescent lights so they could see what they were doing. But when they left, old Ben James was stuck in the dark with nothing but a two-dollar flashlight and a bright moon."

"Well, he used his flashlight to search all over the house, from the hallway through the bedrooms and the den and then into the kitchen. He couldn't find that padlock anywhere. He started searching the dining room, and that's when his batteries went dead and the house went black."

"Ben decided to go back to the patrol car and get spare batteries. His eyes weren't used to the dark, so he felt his way along the living room walls and edged slowly toward the hallway. He could just barely make out the double doorway when the last of the moon's light flooded the hall and – ka-*BUMP!*" Charlotte thumped her open hand on the hood of the car, making Jerry and Nina jump. "Both French doors closed shut at the same time."

"Ben was thinking that the wind must have blown them closed. Just as he reached out to push them back open, his eyes picked up movement on the other side of the glass. He looked up and saw a woman with long, frost-white hair and a shawl, and bare, bloody feet. She was standing there, shimmering, looking at the front door and not moving."

"Then the sun broke over the horizon and the sky got light enough to see the floors and walls. Light enough to see that the barefoot lady was gone – if she'd ever really been there, that is."

"A moment later, the hall was lit up by the dawn sky, and right where Ben had seen the ghostly feet was the county's high-priced padlock. Sitting right out there on the hallway floor, right out in the open. Right where he'd been standing a little over an hour earlier as he was helping the coroner."

Jerry stopped her. "Wait a minute! Abbie turned into a ghost and gave the lock back? I'm sorry, but that really is a stretch."

"You don't believe in ghosts, do you?" Charlotte asked him.

"No. No, I don't."

"May I ask why not?"

"Because when you die, you're gone. You don't come back."

"Why? Simply because you're dead? Do you know what death is, Jerry?" There was a softness to her question that belied the subject matter

"Death is the end of life," he said without hesitating.

"Is that the best you can do? All right, then tell me what 'life' is."

"What do you mean, 'life'? In terms of reproduction or what?"

"Life," she coaxed, drawing out the word.

"I...I don't understand."

"It's a simple question." Charlotte stood directly in front of him. "Life. What is it? Why are you alive?" She reached out and took Nina's hand in her own and asked, "Why is *she* alive?"

"This is silly. The answer is obvious. Life is...life is when...well..." he stammered.

Jerry turned to Nina for help but she didn't have an answer, either. "Well, I'll be damned."

Charlotte smiled. "That's all right. It was a trick question. Life is a secret. You're not allowed to know what it is. But life and death are pages from the same book. One is meaningless without the other. If you don't know what life is about, you can't possibly understand death."

"And ghosts? Are they real? What are they?" Nina asked.

"Oh, young lady, it doesn't matter whether you believe in ghosts. They're not offended either way. Just don't be so quick to dismiss what happened to Ben James inside that house."

"I'd like to talk to Ben about that night," Nina said.

Charlotte shook her head. "I don't think that would do any good. I'm the only one he's ever told his story to, and he won't even speak to me any more."

For several seconds, nobody knew what to say. Finally, Nina asked, "Miss Montgomery, is Abbie still in the house? *Our* house? Is she a ghost?"

Charlotte shook her head. "I can't answer that."

Nina seemed deflated. "But, we saw her."

"We saw *something*," Jerry said.

"I can't account for what you saw. Peoples' eyes can play tricks on them, making them see what's not there. And sometimes, blinding them to what's been right in front of them all along. Forgive me, I really must be going." Charlotte released Nina's hand and turned to walk away.

Jerry fished the car keys out of his pocket and opened the passenger door for Nina. She sat, but before pulling her legs inside she turned and asked Charlotte, "Can we give you a ride somewhere?"

"No, thank you just the same. I don't have very far to go." There was more behind her words than simple gratitude for the offer. There was a promise, a gentle invitation of sorts. Or perhaps it was permission.

Made in the USA
Middletown, DE
26 August 2015